HOUSE

KENDALL RYAN

The House Mate

Copyright © 2017 Kendall Ryan

Copy Editing by

Pam Berehulke

Cover Design by

Sara Eirew

About the Book

What's sexier than a bad boy? A badass man who's got his shit together.

Max Alexander is nearing thirty-five. He's built a successful company and has conquered the professional world, but he's never been lucky in love. Since he's focused so much time on his business and raising his daughter, adulting has come at the expense of his personal life.

His social skills are shit, his patience is shot, and at times, his temper runs hot.

The last thing he has time for is the recently single, too-gorgeous-for-her-own-good young woman he hires to take care of his little girl. She's a distraction he doesn't need, and besides, there's no way she'd be interested. But you know what they say about assumptions?

Chapter One

Max

In thirty-four years, I hadn't found a woman yet who could handle me.

My buddies teased me that I had the attention span of a gnat, and while that wasn't true—I had a successful ten-year career in the US Army as a Ranger, and over the last few years I'd built my business into something I could be proud of—I let them go on thinking it. No, there wasn't a damn thing wrong with my focus or level of commitment. Once I decided on something, I was all in.

It was just the idea of being tied down to the same woman day after day—well, let's just say it didn't hold a candle to my freedom. I liked things the way they were. I was free to come and go as I pleased, work long days when business called for it, and take off for a weekend away when the mood struck. I enjoyed my life just the way it was, and I had no plans to change that anytime soon.

"How long's it been since you've been laid?" my good friend and employee Matt asked, grinning at me over the rim of his pint glass with a crooked smile.

My life was simple, and I cherished simple. I didn't

do complicated. Didn't do messy relationships or complex emotions. I was the center of my world and that was just fine with me. I knew it was selfish, but that's just the way things were.

Realizing Matt was actually waiting for me to reply, I muttered out a curse and took a sip of my own beer.

"You've been a crabby asshole at work lately," he added for emphasis.

Christ, he has the discretion of a crackhead in need of a fix. "You do understand I'm your boss, correct?" I glared at him, but he merely flipped me the middle finger. *The dick.*

We were seated at the bar of our favorite local hangout after a long work week. The Fireside Lodge served the best cheeseburgers and the coldest beer in town, and we found ourselves parked right here most Fridays. I was almost surprised the owner hadn't marked these stools as reserved with all the time we spent on them.

"Thank fuck someone had the balls to bring that up," Zach muttered under his breath.

"You draw the short straw?" I asked Matt. They

weren't generally the type to pry into my personal life, but they never hesitated to point out my foul mood.

Despite their annoying probing, they were both pretty good guys. They'd worked for me since I started my construction business on a wing and a prayer three years ago. They stood by me, agreeing to work for less than they were worth until I could afford to pay them more. Now we all did pretty well, but then again, we worked our asses off, so it was all relative.

"Seriously, man. You could use a woman in your life," Matt said, gazing down into his half-empty beer glass.

"Or at least in your bed," Zach added.

My life? That was a big fat no-fucking-thank-you. But my bed? That wasn't the worst idea they'd ever had. I tried to remember the last time I'd had the pleasure of a woman's company. To be fair, it had been a little while, maybe a couple of months, and damn if I was going to admit it to them, but there was a chance they were right.

"I'll take that under advisement," I mumbled, trying not to stroke their egos too much.

"Good, 'cause there's a cute little number giving you the eye over there," Matt said, nudging my ribs with his elbow.

His gaze drifted over toward the pool tables in the back of the bar, and mine followed. A blonde with heavy eyeliner and dressed in a pair of cut-off shorts and a red tank top that was cut dangerously low to reveal the edges of a lacy push-up bra stood with her hip out, staring me down. She wasn't exactly my type, but my dick didn't care. He'd just heard the suggestion of sinking into warm, wet pussy tonight, and he was all in.

Taking a deep breath, I pulled my gaze away, just in time to see the men flanking me sharing a conspiratorial smile. *Assholes.*

Thirty minutes later, I had the blonde in the cab of my truck and was headed for my place.

When we arrived at my house a few minutes later, I squinted at the beat-up sedan parked in my driveway. *That wasn't there when I left this morning.* I parked on the other side of the driveway and climbed out of the truck.

"Stay put for second," I said to the blonde and she nodded, her glossy red lips parting in a smile.

I walked around to the driver's side of the sedan just in time to watch a woman climb out of the car. Dark blond hair hung down, partially obscuring her face, but I'd recognize those bouncy curls anywhere.

"Jenn?" I asked, stopping in my tracks. We'd dated for a few months a couple of years ago, but I hadn't seen her since.

Our awkward breakup was part of the reason I avoided relationships now. She'd been ready for something more: commitment, stability . . . matrimony. I wasn't. The memory of our last conversation still stung. A fun three-month-long fling was snubbed out with a few curt words.

"Aren't you ever going to want to settle down?" she'd asked.

"Probably not."

I'd been cold. But at least I'd been honest.

"Hey, Max." Her voice was emotionless and flat.

I wasn't sure what I was expecting, but if she was here out of the blue, it was probably for a reason.

"What's going on? Is everything all right?" I shot a

quick glance at my date for the evening through the windshield. Her smile had fallen, and she was watching us with rapt interest.

Jenn opened the door to the backseat and lifted out an infant car seat—with a sleeping baby inside.

What the fuck?

My heart rate tripled and my stomach knotted.

"Jenn?" My voice cracked.

"She's yours." Jenn set the infant carrier at my feet and took a step back.

I didn't look down. Truthfully, I couldn't bring myself to look at the baby because I was scared of what I might see. Could she really be mine? Did she look like me? That wasn't possible—was it? I was still watching Jenn, still trying to figure out what in the fuck was happening.

Another uneasy look toward my truck revealed that the blonde's eyes were glued to the scene in front of her, her lips parted in surprise.

"You can have a test done if you want, but she's yours." Jenn wiped a stray tear from her cheek and reached back inside the car for a duffel bag, which she set next to the carrier. "I'm sorry. I just can't do this anymore."

I heard her voice but couldn't process her words. "What are you saying? What are you talking about?"

"I can't handle it, Max. I thought I could, but it turns out I can't. She's yours, so you take her." Jenn's voice trembled as she bent and whispered something to the little girl who was still sound asleep. Then she climbed back into her car and started backing out of my driveway.

"Jenn!" I roared, waving my arms at her. She threw her car into drive and stepped on the gas so hard, her tires gave a little screech, and then she was gone.

Pulling a deep breath into my lungs wasn't as effective as I'd hoped. It felt like there was a lead weight sitting on my chest. I felt frozen to this spot in my driveway, unsure what the next play was, or how I'd even found myself in this game.

The blonde climbed out of my truck and came to stand beside me, looking down at the baby who had slept through the entire thing.

"What an adorable little girl. Is she your niece or something?"

I looked down at the baby for the first time. Her tiny eyelids fluttered, and she stretched one footie-pajama-covered leg before letting it fall slack once again. I was hit by the sudden urge to get her inside the house, to take her in out of the cool night air.

"No. She's mine." I lifted the carrier and held it protectively in front of me. *Mine.* That word sent a small panic racing through me. "What am I going to do now?" I said more to myself than to her. Or maybe it was a question meant for the universe, because my life as I knew it just got flipped inside out.

Blondie shrugged. "I have to pee."

The three of us headed inside, and I set the baby carrier on the living room floor and pointed out the hall bath.

Once she was done, she marched up to me and rose on her tiptoes to press a kiss to my cheek. "I guess tonight's a no-go."

I nodded. "Something like that."

"I'll grab an Uber. You better get her put to bed," Blondie said, fishing her phone out of her tiny denim shorts.

I inwardly groaned. Sex had been the only thing on my mind five minutes ago, and now it wasn't going to happen. Maybe not ever again. I groaned once more.

"There," she said, punching some buttons on her phone. "I'll be out of your hair in five minutes."

Blondie kissed my cheek again and went to wait outside on the porch while I tried not to have a panic attack. What in the fuck was I supposed to do now?

I made a pillow fort on my bed, blocking all the edges, and then attempted to get the baby out of her car seat. That five-point harness was serious. She was sleeping, not skydiving, but whatever. When she was finally free, I lifted her out and laid her down in the center of the bed. I'd take the guest room. The sheets were dusty in there, and I didn't want her sleeping on them. I didn't know much of anything about babies, but I knew their skin and lungs were probably more sensitive than my man-hide was.

Once she was settled, I opened the duffel bag that

Jenn had dropped off with her. Inside was a fuzzy pink blanket, some tiny clothes, a sippy cup, diapers, wipes, and a folded sheet of paper. I opened the note and looked down at Jenn's neat handwriting.

Max,

I know this comes as a surprise. I'm sorry to just dump her on you like this, but I know you can handle it. I know you thought you couldn't, or maybe you just didn't want the responsibility, but you're the strongest man I know. You'll be better at this than I was. I'm sure of it.

Her name is Dylan. She just turned one, her birthday was Sunday. She takes a nap after lunch and she loves baths. Thank you.

With love,

Jenn

I flipped the page over. *That was it?* There were no instructions? No manual, no nothing. I knew the running joke was that men didn't read instructions, but believe me, these I would have at least glanced at.

The fact that Jenn had named her Dylan made something clench inside my chest. Bob Dylan was my favorite musician and Jenn knew that—she used to tease me about it. Said my taste in music was from another century. I realized that her choice in name was a way to pay homage to me. If she was willing to do that, then why keep the pregnancy from me? Why hide the fact that she was having my baby?

My gaze drifted back over to the baby . . . *my daughter.* That would take some getting used to.

I had no idea what I was going to do, but I hoped the morning would bring some clarity.

***

I heard the crunch of tires on my gravel driveway and looked out the front window. *Thank God Tiffany's here.*

I was wired after three cups of coffee and had been pacing my living room for the past thirty minutes.

Tiffany had been my personal assistant for going on three years. She made sure all the bills got paid on time, the supplies were ordered for jobs, and most importantly, she kept me in line. She was a problem solver, and so even if this was supposed to be her day off, I needed her.

As usual, Tiffany let herself inside. "What's going on?" she asked, toeing off her shoes at the front door. Working so closely together these last few years meant we were practically family. At least, that was how I viewed our relationship.

Before I could answer, her gaze landed on Dylan, who was sitting on my living room floor watching the Saturday morning cartoons just like I used to do as a kid. Only these weren't the cartoons I remembered. They were too violent and had crude humor, so we'd have to work on finding something more suitable.

"Max?" Tiffany said, her voice rising like my name was a question.

"Yeah. I know. You better sit down."

Her brows jumped and she lowered herself onto the couch, her gaze still on the little girl. "Is she . . . yours?"

"Yes."

Tiffany swallowed. "Jenn?"

She knew all about my failed attempt at a relationship. In fact, Tiffany had even played the role of a rebound at one point. After my breakup with Jenn, Tiffany had kissed me at our company Christmas party and had grabbed the front of my jeans, or rather, what was inside. And for the next ninety seconds, I'd let myself think with my dick—towing her into my office and kissing her back. But then I'd come to my senses. I'd let her down carefully, wanting to preserve our working relationship.

Rubbing a hand over the back of my neck, I sighed. "She dropped her off last night. Said she couldn't do it anymore."

Tiffany placed her hand over her chest. "Wow. I'm going to need something stronger than coffee this morning," she joked.

I sat down on the couch beside her. "You know I'm not good about asking for help."

"No, you're not. But you're going to need it."

I nodded again.

"Whatever you need, Max. I'm here."

I swallowed, scrubbing a hand over my face. My gaze wandered down to Dylan, who was still absorbed in the show. I'd changed her diaper when she woke up this morning, given her dry Cheerios and filled her sippy cup with milk. She'd watched me curiously while I drank my coffee, but she didn't cry and didn't ask for her mama, which was both a relief and made me sad. I didn't know what I was doing, but so far, so good.

"You know I don't like to admit it when I need help, but I'm not going to be able to manage everything, not with work too. I've thought about it, and I don't want to stick her in a day care where she doesn't know anybody."

Tiffany nodded.

The truth was I felt bad for the baby after being abandoned by her mom, and I felt all kinds of guilty that I didn't know about her in her first year of life.

"So you're going to keep her . . . here."

"Yeah."

Tiffany smiled at me and patted the back of my hand. "Maybe it's time for a fresh start, Max. Maybe this is the universe's way of intervening. I really think this could be the beginning of something great."

"You're right."

"I am?" She grinned at me.

"Yeah. Everything will work out, right? I'm going to hire a nanny. I'm willing to pay top dollar, but I want the best of the best. It's the perfect solution. I can work from home sometimes so I'm around more, and Dylan won't have to be shuffled from place to place."

Her eyebrows pinched together. "Oh, okay. Yeah. That's a good idea. The only thing is you're going to need to pray that she can start ASAP. Most people want to give a two-week notice to their current employer."

Tiffany was right. All I could do was hope that somewhere out there, the universe was at work putting all the pieces into play so my puzzle would fit together.

Chapter Two

Addison

"You just need a fresh start. A do-over," my best friend, Lara, said as she flopped onto the couch I'd been crashing on for the past week. She wrestled my blanket away from me before tossing a white paper bag from the drugstore into my lap.

"What's all this?" I grumbled, rubbing the sleep from my eyes.

"The start of your new and improved life."

I rifled inside the bag and pulled out a box of purple hair dye, a bottle of bright pink nail polish, and about a dozen fashion magazines—all with headlines screaming things like the number of ways I could "Get Him to Beg for More."

As if.

I held up the box of hair dye and raised my eyebrows. "Seriously?"

"Sometimes new starts are drastic. I figured it was worth a try," she said with a wink.

"And that if I didn't want to dye my hair, this color would look cute mixed in with your newly blond locks?" I smirked.

It was the truth. With her blunt platinum bob and her bright gray eyes, Lara would look seriously fierce with some purple streaks. My regular old brown hair, on the other hand? Not so much.

"You know me too well." She grabbed one of the magazines from my lap and flipped open the front cover. "I thought we might just look at these to get some fresh ideas. Think outside the box and focus on something other than, you know." She flipped another page, aggressively avoiding eye contact with me. "The incident."

Right.

The incident.

That was the gentle way we'd begun referring to the complete and utter collapse of my personal life. Of course, I tended to opt mentally for the more fitting title of *Addison's Personal Apocalypse*, but that was a little too wordy.

Not that I had anyone to blame for the destruction

of my life other than myself since it all started when I turned my boyfriend gay.

I know what you're thinking—that's not possible. But let me assure you, it most certainly is.

I am living proof.

I wanted to ask if Lara had partially gotten these magazines in the hope that, if I learned how to make a man beg for more in ten easy steps, my next boyfriend wouldn't fall victim to my personal doom.

Instead, I opted to ignore the magazines altogether.

"I'm keeping the nail polish."

She nodded. "Thought it was your style. Now, come on, flip open a magazine and get to studying. We're fixing your life, and it starts today."

I let out a little snort. "Do you have a time machine?"

"Stop it." Lara waved a page with a quiz at me. "How about we figure out your best colors. You hold swatches up to your skin to see if you're an autumn or a spring or—"

I flopped back on the couch. "You don't have to do this, you know. You're already being too nice by letting me stay here."

Lara rolled her eyes like she always did when I mentioned it. "It's no problem. I know you would have done the same if something like that had happened to me."

"Except it wouldn't." I punched the pillow behind my head and turned to face her. "You play it smart. Stay single, stay away from guys—"

"As if that's a choice," Lara said with an eye roll.

"It's a good one. Then you don't end up here, on your best friend's couch with no apartment, no job, and no mojo." I blew a strand of dull brown hair away from my face, and Lara gripped my wrist.

"It's not your fault. You just didn't know."

Didn't know was an understatement.

I was shocked. Floored. Frigging destroyed.

Of course, in hindsight, there were little things. Like, for example, he'd wanted to try a few things that were . . . less than usual for me in the bedroom, but I'd chalked that up to my relative inexperience. Half the stuff he asked for I'd never even heard of, and even though I did my best to please him, I was considerably less than masterful with the strap-on he'd gotten me as a birthday gift. It felt like every time I tried to step outside my carefully constructed sexual comfort zone, he walked away frustrated, and I walked away feeling a little less like a woman, a little less like a person, really, because I couldn't seem to give him what he needed.

Maybe if I'd had these magazines then, I would have been able to make things turn out differently.

Maybe. But maybe not.

Holding my breath, I thought back to the night I'd woken to find an empty space in the bed beside me. I heard the low hum of the television and the telltale creaking of our ancient hand-me-down couch. Anxious to see if my boyfriend was all right, I'd crept into the living room only to find him sitting in the middle of the sofa with his hand stuffed down the front of his sweatpants, gay porn playing at low volume on the TV.

"What the hell?" I'd asked.

"What the hell with you?" he'd said, somewhat

nonsensically. He ripped his hand away from his crotch like someone had electrocuted him, his eyes wide.

"Is that . . . is this what you're into? Are you—" I'd sputtered, confused and hurt but hoping there was an explanation.

"God, Addison." He sneered at me. "Don't be so closed-minded. Fantasies are different from reality. You think just because you dress up as a slutty nurse I feel like you want to bang a doctor?"

"Wait, what?" I ran a hand over my face, still baffled by his logic, but also fighting tears. "No, but . . ." I motioned to the television.

"It's no different. I would think my girlfriend could understand that."

I choked on my words, trying to find the right ones, until finally I said, "Okay. Just give me a little time to process this, all right?"

Surely, if I loved him, this should be no issue. I was young. Hip. A cool girlfriend.

After that night, I'd done some googling and discovered that I wasn't alone. He was right; plenty of guys did watch gay porn and weren't gay. In a way, that was comforting, and again I threw myself into trying to make him happy. I bought things online and looked up different techniques, and still every time I walked away a little bit more broken than I had been before. A little bit more unsure about myself and my ability to please him.

I glanced at Lara, wondering if she was recalling the whole mess too, but her eyes were practically glued to an illustration of a cartoon man, complete with little arrows to highlight the erogenous zones.

I flicked through the glossy pages filled with fragrance ads and photos of happy women crunching on salads, stopping on a numbered list of ways to "Empower Your Inner Goddess."

Maybe if I'd done that with Greg, I could have escaped with some of my self-confidence and dignity intact instead of being the last sucker to know.

"Okay, fine, what the hell. I'll give it a try," I muttered.

I skimmed through the list, which mainly focused on different ways to think about your underwear throughout the day, then glanced up at Lara. "I think my inner goddess is even more boring than my outer goddess."

She made a *tsk*ing noise. "Stop, would you?"

The next section focused on work—how to tell your boss what you wanted, how to stay sexy on the job, what kind of underwear to wear to the office.

My stomach clenched at the word *office*.

"Do you think this career advice actually works?" I asked, trying to keep the edge of panic out of my voice. Not only had I lost Greg, but I had been working with him in the café he'd opened a little over two years ago. At the time, I'd told myself that I was sacrificing my dreams to help build his, and then, once his goal was realized, we'd find time for me. That we'd be partners in making *our* dreams come true.

As it happened, though, I was pretty sure I'd just been the best source of cheap labor.

Even now, I could hardly remember what my dreams were back then. As a teen and young adult, I'd spent every summer working at summer camps, teaching the kids sign language and arts and crafts. During school, I always worked in a day care and volunteered at an after-school center.

I guess that was what had always come naturally to me. I talked to Greg a couple of times about it. I definitely asked him once, when and if we ever got married, whether we might find time for me to go back to college for my teaching certificate. Eventually, it would have been nice to be a speech therapist. But now . . .

Now I was twenty-five and broke. And I didn't think my underwear—no matter how flashy—was going to make my professional dreams a reality. I was going to have to find a job. Fast.

"What's the worst breakup you ever had?" I asked Lara.

She blinked, closing her magazine for a moment. "I thought we weren't talking about—"

"We're not. I'm asking about *you*."

She wrinkled her pert nose, her heart-shaped lips tilting to the side. "Probably Tim Erickson. My first love in high school. He dumped me right before prom."

"How did you get back on your feet? What did you do?" I asked.

"I ate a lot of Chinese food."

I nodded.

"Then I went to prom with someone really hot."

I raised my eyebrows. "Oh?"

"Yeah, my cousin." She laughed. "But my ex didn't know that. Oh, and I got a part-time job. Got a new boyfriend out of that too."

"Hmm." I placed the magazine in front of me, then sat up cross-legged on the pull-out.

"Will you hand me my computer?" I asked.

"Uh-oh, I see gears turning. What are you up to?"

"Maybe fresh starts have some merit. I'm going to get started. Now, let's see. I have to—" I opened a new tab on the Internet browser. "Find a new apartment." I opened another tab. "Get new furniture." I opened another tab. "Buy food for said apartment." Another tab. "Find a job."

Lara snatched the computer away from me. "Maybe let's focus on one thing at a time. You look like you're about to hyperventilate."

I couldn't deny it. My chest was so tight that it hurt to breathe. "Okay, fine."

"Now, what kind of job do you want?" Lara asked, her voice therapist-calm.

"Something better than the damn café." I sniffed. "If I never smell coffee again, it'll be too soon."

"The hell you say," Lara hissed. She was a coffee lover.

"Fine. Okay, for real, though. Maybe something with kids?"

"That's good. You're great with kids." Lara typed furiously and then scanned the entries on the jobs website while I stared at the laptop screen. "Oh my God, I found the perfect one. You're never going to believe it."

She swiveled the screen around and I glanced at the listing. It was a full-time nanny position. A single father was hoping someone could become a live-in nanny for his twelve-month-old little girl.

"Live-in?" I read aloud.

"Isn't it perfect?" Lara asked. "Room and board, and a job to boot. Like all your prayers have been answered.

He wants someone nurturing and attentive, loving and patient. That's you all day."

"That's nice of you to say." I read over the description again, then my eyes widened when I reached the salary. It was more—much more, in fact—than I'd been making at the café. And with none of that money going toward rent . . .

"This is sort of a no-brainer, huh?" I asked.

Lara grinned, and I clicked on the listing's e-mail address, hoping that this was exactly as perfect as it seemed.

Despite myself, excitement and hope bubbled up inside my chest, and I tapped away at the keyboard with a thrill of newfound energy.

Everything could be different.

All I needed to do was land this job . . .

Chapter Three

Max

Somehow I did it. I'd survived my first three nights alone with my daughter. My entire house was trashed and we'd eaten out for almost every meal, but hey, this was survival. Those restaurants with carry-out specials where you park in a designated spot and they bring your food out to you? Those were my new favorite thing.

I hadn't slept much, my work had suffered, and it was all ten times harder and more overwhelming to take care of a small person than I ever imagined it would be. But I was alive and so was Dylan. That had to count for something, right?

Dylan was currently playing with a set of plastic measuring cups and spoons on the kitchen floor. We needed to go shopping. Groceries, toys—you name it, I probably needed it. But I didn't want to fill my house with plastic junk she didn't need. I wasn't going to be one of those crazy helicopter parents. I was going to be a cool dad. I wanted to raise a little girl who knew how to use tools, not one who was obsessed with becoming a Disney princess.

The doorbell rang, and I could have dropped to my knees with joy at that moment. It meant Addison Lane, one of the nanny candidates, was here for her interview.

Surveying my living room, I inwardly groaned. It looked like an M-4 had detonated in here. Stray clothes, dirty dishes, and toys were scattered everywhere.

Shit.

Since it was too late to do anything about it, I pushed it from my brain and picked up Dylan from where she was playing on the floor to go and answer the door.

I wasn't a religious man, but when my hand met the doorknob, I paused just before pulling it open and said a silent prayer. *Dear God, please let her be nice and normal and have a deep, unending love for children.* Her résumé and qualifications were stellar, so it was going to come down to gut feeling today. If she was as sweet and nurturing as she'd been on the phone, she could have the job.

Pulling open the door, I looked out at the woman standing on my porch.

"Oh, hi," the brunette said, turning to face me.

When she turned, I felt like I'd been punched in the

chest. Desire swamped the air between us, and lust burned low in my groin. She was pretty—a girl-next-door type with high cheekbones, a full mouth, a lush and perky rack, wide brown eyes fringed in black lashes, and curves to the moon and back.

Fuckity fuck. This was not a good start.

"You have such a beautiful piece of property," she said, twisting her hands in front of her.

I looked at the yard, admiring the view, trying to take a moment to cool myself down. The property was the whole reason I chose to build here when I moved back home after leaving the military. Something about it felt serene to me, the way the huge old oak and pecan trees in the yard sheltered the house from the road, and moss grew in the shade beneath them, but I was surprised she felt the same way. Most people didn't even notice, or at least they didn't comment on it.

"I'm sorry. How rude of me not to introduce myself. I babble when I get nervous. I'm Addison."

She was nervous? I thought I was the only one with a heart jackhammering out of my chest.

I stuck out my hand and shook her delicate one. "Max Alexander. And this is Dylan."

Addison's full lips pulled into a happy grin. Dylan smiled back at her, waving her chubby fist in greeting.

Dammit. I should have closed the door in her face the second I saw her smoldering-hot curves. Or maybe I should have included in the ad that I would only consider candidates with at least two hairy moles on their face. As it was, though, I'd done neither, and was therefore forced to watch the silent bond forming between this gorgeous stranger and my daughter.

It happened in the space of an instant. So quickly that, if I hadn't been looking, I might have missed it. But now there was no denying it. Both of Dylan's arms were outstretched, and she was gurgling for a chance to get a closer look.

And, frankly, so was I.

Addison glanced at me, and I noticed that she had a dimple in her right cheek to match Dylan's. Still grinning, she motioned to the baby. "Do you mind if we get acquainted?"

"Not at all." I shook my head and took a step inside, ushering her into the foyer.

Addison swooped in, expertly transferring Dylan from my arms to her own, and that singular instant of skin-on-skin contact was enough to make my cock stand up at attention. I opened my mouth to ask her a question, but before I got the chance, she was sinking to the floor, letting Dylan down to sit in front of her.

"Hi, little miss." Addison waved her hand again, and when Dylan gripped her finger, shaking it happily, she cooed, "You're awfully friendly, aren't you?"

Was she? I racked my brain, trying to remember if Dylan had acted this way with anyone else she'd come into contact with in the past few days. I couldn't remember her crying when strangers addressed her, but she'd never begged to be held by them either.

"So, tell me about her," Addison said, craning her neck to look up at me. I was painfully aware that, from this angle, I could see straight down the front of her shirt, enough to see the lush curve of her skin and the top of her lacy pink bra.

I sank to my knees next to them to keep from

perving out on my potential nanny even more.

Truthfully, I had no idea what to fucking say, so I just winged it. "Well, I'm trying to raise her to be independent. I don't want her dreaming about finding some white knight to take care of her. I want her to be practical and strong in her own right."

Addison nodded, and a strand of silky brown hair fell in front of her face. "That's so great. What sort of things does she like to do? Go to the park? Listen to stories at bedtime?"

I opened my mouth and closed it again, my mind blank. In three days, I'd learned how to soothe Dylan's temper and how to change her diaper. I'd finally come to recognize when she was hungry and when she needed to sleep, but in terms of her personality . . . well, that sort of thing took time.

And time was the one thing we hadn't had together. At least, not until now.

"How about we focus on the particulars of the job first?" I asked.

Addison frowned slightly, her cheeks reddening, but

she nodded again. "Sure, sounds good."

She giggled as Dylan blew a spit bubble at her, and I forced myself to focus on the task at hand.

"Okay, so I've looked over your résumé and everything seems in order. You have a long history of child care for someone so young."

Her eyes softened. "I really like kids a lot. Always have. It's one of those things, you know?"

"I guess it is." I nodded. "So, this job would be a little different from summer camp and day care. It's a full-time commitment, meaning that if Dylan gets up in the middle of the night—"

"I'm on the job," she cut in with a bright smile. "My goal would be to make your life easier and ensure that you feel Dylan is happy and safe at all times. Does she often wake up in the middle of the night?"

I paused. *Maybe?*

"No. Not usually." Hoping Addison didn't notice my hesitation, I briskly continued. "I have a housekeeper who comes on Saturdays, and though I usually work out of the home, I'll sometimes need you to take care of Dylan while

I'm in my home office, and ensure that she doesn't distract me."

"Not a problem." She tweaked Dylan's nose, and the baby squealed with delight.

"Food and board are included, plus your salary, and you would be provided with a card for your grocery expenses and any necessities you might need for Dylan's care."

"Wow, you really thought of everything," Addison said, and Dylan let out another shriek of glee.

I cleared my throat. "Do you have any questions for me?"

"Um, where would I be staying?"

"Right." I got to my feet, and holding my breath, held out my hand for her. As she took it, allowing me to help her to her feet, I hoped to God she couldn't feel the tense pounding of my pulse in my fingers. "I'll show you."

She bent over, and I looked away to avoid staring at the curve of her ass as she scooped Dylan into her arms.

Where would *she* stay? Where would *I* stay? I'd been around this woman for less than twenty minutes and I was already harder than a fucking baseball bat. Damn it all, if she was living with me, I'd have to sleep in a tent in the backyard just to keep myself away from her.

Although, at the rate I was going, I could just sleep in the tent in my pants.

I bit back a groan and tried to think. Maybe I could pretend to have impossible standards and tell her I was going to keep looking, or maybe . . .

I turned to find Dylan still giggling in Addison's arms, her bright eyes shining as she studied the woman holding her, and everything else stopped. This choice wasn't about me. It had to be about Dylan. About what Dylan needed, what she wanted.

And she clearly wanted Addison.

"This is Dylan's room." I opened the first door at the top of the stairs, but not enough for Addison to see that it was practically empty except for the diaper bag Dylan's mother had left with me. Quickly, I moved to the next door and opened it. "This would be your room."

It had been a guest room before, and it bore all the neutral, indistinct furniture and linens of a room without personality. I glanced at her over my shoulder, and she nodded.

"Wow, a king-sized bed. I've never had one of those." She let out a low whistle.

"Then next door," I said as I pointed, hating myself, "is mine."

Which means only one wall will separate us at night.

I clenched my fist inside my pocket. "The door on the opposite wall is my office, and the door at the end of the hall is the guest bath, which you and Dylan will share."

"Great." She nodded. "And in terms of compensation?"

I breathed deep. I could cut in half the salary that I'd listed online. That might send her running for the hills. But then I glanced at Dylan again and remembered Addison's sterling résumé.

"Ideally, I'd like to go with what's listed in the ad you responded to. We can talk about more once you've gone through a trial period and we see how things are going."

"That all sounds great."

I told her about her health benefits and vacation time, and when I was done with my spiel, she gave me another enthusiastic nod.

"So, I guess there's only one thing left," I said.

This is all about Dylan, I reminded myself. *Not you. Her.*

I let my gaze sweep over Addison one last time. Maybe if I pretended she had something terribly wrong with her, it might make it easier.

"When can you start?" I asked.

"I got the job?" She grinned, snuggling Dylan a little closer to her. The baby snatched a lock of her hair and yanked it, but if Addison noticed, she didn't show it.

"Absolutely. If you don't mind, it would be great if you could start tomorrow. I know it's short notice, but—"

"No, no, it's fine. Completely fine." She handed Dylan back to me. "This is going to be great. I'm so excited."

"We are too." I nodded. "So we'll see you at eight tomorrow?"

"You've got it."

Boy, did I ever. And bad.

With a few more parting words, she hustled out the door, and then I set Dylan in her high chair and got down to making us lunch.

"It's going to be great, kiddo," I muttered, giving Dylan a pep talk that was clearly meant for myself.

Tomorrow, everything was going to be easier. Once Addison was here, things would go back to being about as calm as before Dylan arrived.

Almost as if she'd read my mind, my tiny daughter let out a peal of maniacal laughter that sent a chill straight down my spine.

Famous last words.

Chapter Four

Addison

I let out a slow, calming breath and then forced myself to hold in my squeak of glee when I opened the door.

"Guess what?" I swung my arms wide, careful not to fling the bag of takeout in my hand across the room.

Lara turned around, midway through stirring whatever was in the skillet on the stove.

I frowned, my shoulders slumping. "I brought home dinner. I thought it was my night."

Lara shrugged, shooting me a half smile. "Figured you'd be busy, so I made chicken marsala."

I pushed the door closed behind me, practically trembling with excitement.

"But I'm guessing that's not what you came in here all fired up to tell me?" Lara said.

I skirted around the couch, still pulled out from the night before, and set the bag of food on the counter. "No. It's not." The squeak I'd been holding in escaped, sounding like the air coming out of a balloon. "I got the job, and I start tomorrow!"

"Holy shit, yay! That was fast." Lara's eyes widened. "So, what do you think?"

"I think it's perfect. The house is on the cutest little street." I pressed my hand to my heart.

Maxwell Alexander lived in a well-kept two-story brick house tucked back on a deep lot filled with mature trees. It was a very pretty home . . . white brick with black shutters framing the windows, a big front porch, and a bright red front door.

"My favorite thing about it was the trees. It makes you feel safe, like you're hidden away in the woods." Then again, that could have been because symbolically, and maybe literally, I was all about hiding.

But not anymore. I wasn't hiding at this job. There, with baby Dylan, I was going to be my authentic self. I was going to be completely and totally honest.

Except, of course, for one tiny little detail . . .

"All right, girl, relax. You're just working there, you're not getting buried there," Lara said with a chuckle.

I rolled my eyes. "It's just the perfect environment. And this little girl—oh my God, you should see her. She's an absolute dream."

"How can a one-year-old be a dream? They're like screaming little poop machines," Lara said with a shudder.

"She never cried. She came right to me, and she was a complete delight. I think it's going to be perfect."

I let out another long sigh, picturing the untidy living room. Before long, it was going to be cluttered with toys and books, and I would be there with Dylan, taking care of her and doing what I was always meant to do. And then in the evening, I'd make dinner, and Max would come home and . . .

And I would let them enjoy their family time. And stay far away from her hottie of a daddy, Max. Because the new Addison was firmly rooted in reality and aware of everything going on around her.

Lara spooned the chicken, mushrooms, rice, and sauce onto plates, and I grabbed some naan and hummus from the bag I'd brought. We sat together at the tiny table in the corner of the room to eat.

"Tell me, how was your day? I'm totally hogging the spotlight," I said, feeling like a bit of a fraud for not even mentioning how sexy Max was. It was so not relevant, but still.

"No, no," Lara said as she forked her chicken. "My day was nothing to write home about. I want to hear more about you. Go on."

"Well . . ." I searched my brain. "I think he's going to need some help with the baby's room. I don't get the feeling that he has a passion for decorating. But that will be a fun job for me, I think."

"What's he like?" Lara raised her eyebrows. "Cute?"

I shrugged and tried to keep my cheeks from flushing. "Sure. I mean, yeah, I guess."

Lara chewed, then after she swallowed, asked, "How did he end up a single father? Is he divorced or a widower?"

I frowned. "Oh, I, um, didn't ask."

Of course, it had occurred to me to ask, but given my frantic heartbeat and near-panting status when I got within five feet of the guy, I thought it was probably best not to focus too much on how single he was. After all, it was an interview, not a speed date.

"Weird." Lara shook her head. "Men almost never get custody."

"I guess not. I didn't really think about it."

"Too taken with the picturesque neighborhood and hobbit-like forest?" Lara laughed.

"Oh, make your jokes, but I'm telling you, you would be knocked out by this place too. I think I can really make a difference here. Max has this cool philosophy about making sure Dylan—that's the baby—stays down to earth. No Snow White nonsense for her, just a pink tool set and a good strong work ethic."

Lara pursed her lips. "No dress-up?"

"Not the princess kind." I picked off a piece of naan and popped it into my mouth. "I think it's good. Healthy."

"Whatever you say. You're the nanny." She held up her hands in surrender and then retrieved her fork.

"Yeah, I think this could really work out, you know? It could be really, really great," I repeated, then took another bite of my food, although I barely tasted it.

Instead, I was thinking about the house. And Dylan.

And what it was going to be like when tomorrow came and I was all alone there.

With Max.

If he noticed the way I'd looked at him, he definitely wouldn't have given me the job. I had to hope that the charisma pouring off him and the effect of that smoking-hot bod wore off once we spent a few days around each other. Otherwise? I was in big trouble. And I wasn't about to ruin this dream opportunity.

"Are you nervous about living with a strange man?" Lara asked, and I blinked for a minute, certain she could read my mind.

"No, no, of course not. It's professional. Totally professional." I stumbled over the words and Lara smirked.

"I never said it wasn't. Unless you think—"

"No, I don't. I said yesterday, remember? I've sworn off men. I clearly can't be trusted to make the right choices. I was with Greg and then, bam. All my dreams were gone. Two years of my life wasted."

"But we weren't talking about romance, I thought?" Lara asked lightly.

"We're not. I'm just saying—" I shook my head. "Ugh, it came out all wrong."

"So he's hot, huh?" Lara asked, that knowing smirk still mocking me.

I wanted to bang my head against the dining room table. "Yes," I confessed on an exhale. "He's gorgeous. He's tall and tanned and muscular, and he's got that jaw— you know how some guys have that defined jaw?"

"I do." Lara nodded.

"But anyway, I'm not going to get involved with him," I pronounced.

"Because you've sworn off men?"

"And because he's my boss," I sputtered. "Can you imagine the disaster? I'm not going to be homeless and jobless again. Not ever."

Lara shrugged. "Probably a smart move. But are you sure you can resist him?"

I snorted. "Positive," I said with a nod.

Then I thought back to the way he'd looked when he opened the door, his hair all messy, his face in need of a shave, that scowl painted across his full lips, and the bad-boy ink on both forearms. He wasn't like any other man I'd ever seen in real life, and certainly none that I'd dated.

In truth? That was no small part of the appeal. But self-destructive, bad-decision-making Addison was dead and gone.

And she was going to stay that way.

Chapter Five

Max

Ding-dong.

I whirled around just as the toast popped up from the toaster and Dylan shrieked from her high chair.

"What the . . ." I glanced at the clock. It was seven thirty—a full thirty minutes before the nanny was supposed to be here. I hadn't even combed my hair or brushed my teeth yet. And as for the kitchen?

I glanced around, looking for any place where the counter was actually visible.

"Damn," I mumbled, and then plowed my fingers through my hair as I made for the door. When I opened it, I found Addison on the step with a suitcase, her long brown hair swept into a neat ponytail on top of her head.

"Good morning," she chirped.

I'd bypassed my typical morning wood since I'd been awakened by the sounds of the baby screeching, but now, with Addison at the door like the opening shot to a porno flick titled *Naughty Nanny's First Day*, my cock swelled.

"Uh, hi. You're early," I said, stepping aside so she could walk into the foyer. Catching sight of her bag, I scrubbed my hand over my face. "Shit, you probably have stuff you wanted to bring. Should I have sent some movers or—"

She shook her head and held up a hand. "I'm completely fine. I've got everything I need. I'm just going to run my stuff upstairs, and we can get started."

"Perfect," I said, my tone slightly annoyed as she headed for the stairwell beside me while I was careful not to reel around and try to catch a glimpse of that round peach of an ass.

God, five minutes in and I was already acting like a fuck-stick. What was wrong with me?

Dylan squealed again and I rushed for the kitchen, pulling the bread from the toaster and slathering a healthy portion of peanut butter over the browned surface.

"There you go, kid." I set the toast onto the tray of her high chair. "One for you, and one for me."

She reached for my piece, ignoring her own, but I chomped on it, brushing away some of the crumbs I was dropping all over the floor.

Watching Dylan navigate her piece of toast, I was suddenly hit with a wave of worry. *Am I doing the right thing by leaving her here today with a perfect stranger?*

The coffeepot dinged and I made my way over, briefly debating whether to pour one mug or two before realizing there was only one clean mug left, anyway.

"All right, all settled." Addison appeared in the doorway. She was wearing a light blue button-down top with polka dots. It was prim and proper, very Carol Brady—not that Addison was old enough to know who that was.

She glanced around the room and winced, but then covered it quickly with a smile. "I can take it from here." She aimed that grin at Dylan, who cooed in delight. "All I need to know is what Dylan's daily schedule is usually like."

She turned her gaze on me and I frowned, unsure how to respond. "Her schedule?" Dylan was a baby. She didn't exactly have a to-do list.

"Yeah, what kind of routine do you guys have?"

I blinked. "We, um, we're sort of free spirits. Not much of a schedule."

Addison tilted her head slightly, but her expression didn't change from its placid, thoughtful state. "That's cool. Since I'm new around here, Dylan and I can probably develop our own schedule over time. You'll be surprised what a difference routines make for little ones. I'm sure you'll see the improvement."

"I'm sure I will." I glanced at the door, then back at Addison. "Maybe I should stay around since this is your first day? I can work from home while you learn the ropes. I don't want to just toss you in here."

Dylan cackled, and I became uncomfortably aware of the electricity buzzing between Addison and me.

This poor woman must think I'm insane. One minute I'm an asshole, and the next I'm leering at her.

She swept her arm through the air, waving me off. "Don't be silly. You need to work, and Dylan and I need a schedule. It's a perfect arrangement for everyone."

"I left a list of important information on the fridge. Phone numbers too."

Addison nodded. "I appreciate that."

Already, she was wiping away the smudge of peanut butter from Dylan's cheek and clearing the crumbs from her high-chair tray.

"Don't be afraid to use it, all right?" I said, suddenly filled with a strange apprehension at the thought of leaving.

"I won't." She picked up a few errant mugs from the table in front of the wide bay window and plunked them on top of the mound of dishes that filled the sink. "It's almost eight. You should probably get going. Do you need some coffee first?" She motioned to the pot, and I shook my head.

"No, no, I'm fine. That's for you."

She grinned. "Thanks, that's really nice."

"Don't be afraid to call me if something is wrong. My cell is the first number on the list."

"You bet. Don't worry. You have my number, and everything is going to be great," she said encouragingly. The dimple in her cheek made the briefest appearance, and despite myself, my lips split into a matching smile.

"Yeah." I nodded, and I wasn't sure how she did it, but twenty minutes later, she managed to push me out the door of my own house. Before I knew it, I was standing on the steps where she'd been only moments before, staring at my truck and digging in my pocket for my keys.

I had half a mind to walk back in there and read aloud to her everything I'd written down. I was nearly to the point of turning the handle when she appeared with Dylan at the front window, both of them waving me off.

"Bye-bye, Daddy," Addison cooed. "Say bye-bye."

I waved back at them, then trudged toward my truck with a full heart. As I backed out of the driveway, they never moved from where they stood. All the while they waved after me, and I watched them in my rearview mirror until they were only specks.

How could Jenn have left Dylan with me like that when it was making my gut churn just to leave her behind with the nanny? I shook my head, marveling at the oddness of parenthood, and doing my best to ignore the little voice in my head that urged me to turn around and go back home to be with Dylan again.

Maybe that was why the drive to work felt so

exceptionally long. It was like every light tu

all the traffic crawled to a standstill. My only

to the stare at the clock on the dashboard, or wait for my

phone to buzz with news about the baby. I knew that any

second I would get a message asking me to come home,

or telling me that Dylan was sick or . . .

I took a deep breath. My office building was just ahead of me now, and I pulled into my parking space, suddenly overcome with exhaustion.

"Coffee," I muttered to myself. "I've got to get some coffee."

Climbing out of my truck, I pulled my cell from my pocket and glanced at the home screen. It was cheesy, I knew, but Dylan's face stared back at me from the photo I'd taken yesterday and chosen as my wallpaper, a spit bubble still wet on her lips. No messages.

"Probably still having breakfast," I said, then internally scolded myself. I couldn't go through the entire day talking to myself. I wasn't going to become that guy— that nervous parent who left the office at lunchtime because he couldn't stand to be away from his kid.

Dylan was in good hands. I just had to be patient. I

.ould do this.

With all that in mind, I climbed the stairs to my office and managed to only check my cell another four times before opening my door and trudging toward my Keurig. As I popped a K-cup into place, Tiffany hurried through the door, her red hair slightly mussed.

"Damn, I was trying to beat you to the coffeepot." She blew out a shallow breath, then held her chest as it rose and fell in quick succession.

"Did you actually run in here?"

She smiled. "Maybe."

Laughing at herself, she took a seat across from my desk, and we reviewed the notes and agenda for the day. A few times, she paused, and I knew she was on the brink of asking me about Dylan, but either my serious gaze or her own inhibitions stopped her. Whatever the reason was, though, I was grateful for it.

"Okay, I think that's everything," I said, and my phone buzzed against the rustic wood surface of my desk.

Without bothering to excuse myself, I snatched up the phone and thumbed it open. Dylan stared back at me, but this time it wasn't my wallpaper photo—she was in her high chair mixing something in a bright yellow bowl and making a mess of it, her head tossed back in mid-laugh. I scrolled down and read the text.

ADDISON: *Someone likes banana pancakes!*

The text featured a little monkey emoji beneath it, and I smiled.

"Everything all right?" Tiffany asked, and I was surprised to see her still standing there as I looked up.

"Yeah, everything's great."

She cocked her head and then backed away. "All right then, if you're sure."

After she left, I stared at the door, still thinking of Dylan mixing her pancake ingredients. I would never have thought to cook with her or have her help like that, not when she was so young. I'd be too nervous about the stove or her somehow getting to one of the knives . . .

I sipped my coffee, blowing a deep breath out my

nose. Even now, with all these hypothetical worries trampling my thoughts, I felt better than I had in the last three days combined. The panic of being a parent, of being responsible for another person's life, was still there, churning away at the back of my mind, but I was feeling better by the second. Sure, Dylan might get near the stove or the knives when I was around, but I knew Addison would never let that happen. She had a knack. She was a natural at this in a way I wasn't.

And the way she looked at Dylan? Addison was the one thing I knew I didn't have to worry about.

For the next few hours, I timed myself—only allowing myself to glance at my phone every thirty minutes. Even then, I didn't allow myself to text and ask how Dylan was doing. The girls needed time to bond, and I needed to work. God knew I needed to work.

Around two, though, my phone chimed again and I found another picture waiting for me. This time Addison and Dylan were laughing together, each of them holding sparkly Play-Doh in their hands. Had Addison brought toys with her? She didn't have to do that.

My heart melted when I read the message

underneath.

ADDISON: Don't worry, even the sparkles are non-toxic. We're learning not to eat play dough.

I laughed, imagining Dylan's face wrinkling as she tasted the salty concoction. No doubt that was a lesson she was going to hang on to.

I moved to put my phone down, but then it buzzed in my hand and another message appeared.

ADDISON: Hey, what time do you get home from work? I forgot to ask.

I replied quickly, letting her know I'd be home around six, but before I could put the phone down, it buzzed again.

ADDISON: Okay, great. As for dinner . . . do you have any allergies or anything? Anything you don't like?

MAX: You don't have to go grocery shopping.

Her answer came immediately after my response. I'd left her the car seat just in case, but I'd rather her not have to bother with it.

ADDISON: Too late. I'm making dinner, but I need to know if anything is going to kill you first.

I smiled. She had a sense of humor beneath that bubbly persona.

MAX: No mustard, please. Other than that, I'm easy.

Addison sent a little thumbs-up in return.

Grinning, I put the phone down and turned back to

my work, but before I got a chance to fully dive in, my office door opened.

"Hey, you have a minute?" Tiffany peeked around the door and when I nodded, she stepped inside, careful to shut the door behind her.

"I was thinking, the last couple of days have been tough for you. Do you and Dylan want to come over to my place tonight? It might be nice for you to get a home-cooked meal for a change."

"Thanks for the offer, but I actually already have plans."

She rolled her eyes. "No one calls the drive-through at Wendy's 'plans.'"

I laughed. "No. Dylan's new nanny is making us dinner."

"Oh," she said, her voice tight. After a pause, she added, "I'd wondered where that little muffin was today."

I nodded. "Yep, she's home, and happy and safe. But like I said, that was very nice of you to offer. Thanks again."

"Anytime. It's an open invitation." Tiffany hesitated

and then headed back out the door, closing it with a tiny snap.

I threw myself back into work, and at one point, realized that I was humming under my breath.

I patted myself on the back for a job well done. Now that Addison was living in the house and taking care of the baby, everything was going to be perfect.

Chapter Six

Addison

I swept the hair out of my face and stared around the newly cleaned kitchen.

There was no denying it had been an undertaking. What few groceries left in the fridge needed to be cleaned out—and the hazardous waste department was probably a better candidate to do it than I was, but I'd done my best all the same. My arms were sore up to the elbows from scrubbing away at dishes and getting on my knees to tackle the floors, but there was no doubting the place looked better. I might have even gone so far as to say it looked *damned* good.

Now that Dylan was upstairs napping, I finally sank into a chair, ready to search online for the recipe I'd be making for tonight's dinner.

God, that little girl was an angel.

I hoped Max knew how lucky he was to have her. She hadn't thrown a single temper tantrum—not one, all day. Even when she'd been hungry, she waddled into the kitchen and sat in front of her high chair like a patient puppy waiting to go outside.

Playing with her was easy too. She needed to learn to share, but she understood sounds and shapes well for her age, and when we read together, she listened intently to every word. A few times, she'd even added some words of her own—like "bird" or "car" or "horse." But then, on the rare occasion, she'd say "Da-da."

And twice, she'd said "Ma-ma" too.

I didn't know if this was simply because kids learned these words practically in unison—like one couldn't exist without the other—or because maybe because her mother had been in her life at some point?

In the quieter moments, when I was picking up the living room, I searched the photos in the frames along the mantel to find some sign of a woman in Max and Dylan's life, but there was not even the slightest hint of one. Other than a picture of an elderly woman with her arm slung around Max, who was wearing an Army Ranger uniform, there were no women in his pictures at all. They were all photos of his college graduation, campfires with his friends, and beach trips.

There wasn't even a picture of Dylan. Not anywhere.

It was odd. Based on how doting and careful he'd been with her yesterday and this morning, he didn't seem like the kind of guy who was such an egomaniac that he didn't bother to frame pictures of his own daughter. It was possible, of course, that since he was a guy he just hadn't thought to change things around. After all, for all I knew, the pictures he had could have been set up by his mother when he'd first moved in.

Still, it didn't seem right to me. Not really.

I let out a sigh and scrolled down the page, then selected the tastiest-looking picture and glanced at the recipe. With quick, efficient movements, I collected all the ingredients listed and pushed aside the thoughts in my brain that were exploding with curiosity.

I didn't know Max very well. Maybe I was the caregiver for his daughter, but that didn't give me the right to ask personal questions of him.

And yet . . .

What happened when Dylan was old enough to ask me about her mother? Shouldn't I know whether she was out there somewhere, whether she might show up some weekend to take Dylan for a visit and leave me alone in the house with Max?

My mind stalled on that thought, idling to picture what a dinner alone with him might be like. What the evening afterward could bring.

Excitement and anxiety filled my heart in equal measure. Just thinking about being alone with him had me nearly hyperventilating. He was just so ... daunting. When I'd messaged him throughout the day, he'd only responded to direct questions. And then, when I'd made a little joke about not wanting to kill him, even then he'd answered with a serious response. With the stern, impassive look that was always on his face, the worry etched into his features, it was hard not to take him seriously. He was intimidating, and I wasn't even sure why.

But then I would picture him smiling down at his little girl—holding her in those big strong arms covered in ink, and my knees went weak. His presence was like this looming aura that filled any room he was in, and I was swallowed up in it instantly—on eggshells, holding my breath, hanging on to every word . . .

And wanting to ride him like a bull at the rodeo. Not that it matters. Because it definitely does not.

I shook my head and read over the recipe again, but just as I reached for the first ingredient, the front door swung open.

"Max," I gasped, breathless. I'd been so distracted by thoughts of him in his military garb and riding him like a bull that I hadn't even heard his truck pull up.

He grinned at me, and I noticed that his straight white smile slanted a little to one side, making his jaw look that much more rugged and square.

God, what was *with* me and this guy's jaw?

"You're home early." My gaze shot toward the clock. It was barely even four. I stepped into the foyer as he looked around the living room and his eyes went wide.

"You didn't have to do all this." He gestured to the vacuumed carpet and polished furniture.

"It was no trouble," I said. "Really."

"I have a cleaning lady—"

"I know, I know." I waved him off. "But you know, I live here too and I wanted to do my share." I shrugged.

"I prefer a tidy house, anyway."

He walked into the kitchen, and I followed behind him like a hungry puppy following a trail of dog treats. No doubt my face looked just as hungry as one too, now that I got a good look at his backside in his fitted slacks.

I swallowed hard.

"I'm drawing the line," he said. "You are not making dinner. You must be exhausted."

My feet screamed in agreement with him, but I shook my head all the same. "No, absolutely not. I've already got a recipe. You sit down. You've been working all day."

"You're the one who's been working all day." He gestured toward the clean kitchen, and I rolled my eyes.

"The cleaning, sure, but Dylan's no work. It was a great day."

That much was true. Even with all the running and chasing and multi-tasking, Dylan was a joy. I already felt a deep bond with the little girl, and the reward that came from taking care of her? Well, that was a whole hell of a lot better than passing paper coffee cups along to bleary-eyed zombie-like commuters.

"She's still down for her nap, though, so if you go upstairs—"

"I'll be quiet." He nodded. "Look, I'm sorry I'm here earlier than you expected. I couldn't stay away. I was just a little nervous, but I have to say now that I'm impressed."

I blushed, trying not to look as flustered as I felt. Why should his praise feel like I was being given a gold star by a favorite teacher? I knew I'd done a good job, had gone above and beyond the call of duty. And still . . .

Whenever I looked at him I felt like I couldn't breathe.

"Actually, I was going to say you should probably wake her up. If she sleeps much longer, she'll never go to bed tonight," I said.

He nodded, beaming. "All right. I'll go say hello."

He exited the room, and while I listened to his heavy footfalls on the stairs, I finally allowed myself to exhale again. God, one more week of living here and I was going to need an oxygen tank.

Shaking my head at myself for what felt like the millionth time, I set to work on dinner. I'd marinated some steak, and the potatoes were already in the oven. All I had to do was sear the meat and sauté the asparagus, and it would be the perfect masculine meal.

As the vegetables sizzled in their skillet, I set the table, listening to both father and daughter laughing as they said hello to each other again. Apparently, it hadn't taken much doing to get Dylan up—she'd screamed as soon as her bedroom door opened, and I could hear their soft-spoken conversation all the way from the kitchen.

An hour later when the steak was ready, I called for the little family to join me in the kitchen and served the food on the table. I cut Dylan's steak into tiny pieces and mashed her potato while Max set her in her high chair. As we walked past each other, I felt all the air drain from the room again, swallowed up by his very presence.

"You shouldn't have done all this."

My heart sank. I'd wanted him to be impressed, wanted to go above and beyond to make sure this house felt like a home. I'd been so eager to hear his praise, but now I felt like a fool.

Feeling Max's intense stare on me, I focused my attention on making sure Dylan was eating well.

It had been a while since I'd been able to prepare a home-cooked meal like this. Greg was a gluten-free, GMO-free, non-dairy vegan. After taking so much criticism when I had tried to cook for him, I eventually just gave up. It was irrational, but tears filled my eyes and I had to work to blink them away. I'd been here all of one day, and yet Max's approval felt like everything.

"I can do that. Here, let's switch spots," he said, but I waved him off.

"It's fine. If you don't like the meal, I won't be offended." And if he wanted to order a pizza or run out for a burger, what did I care?

"Who said anything about not liking the meal?"

I dared a glance in his direction.

Using his knife and fork, Max cut a big bite of steak and popped it into his mouth. I held my breath while he chewed.

"Eat," he commanded. "After dinner, you've got the rest of the night off. I'll do the dishes and put Dylan to bed."

"I can't let you do that," I said, but his gaze turned

stern.

"I meant what I said before. You worked all day; you deserve some down time."

"But you worked too. You need—"

"Let me worry about what I need."

His declaration cut off any chance of further discussion, and I settled back into my food was renewed vigor. Partly because I was starving and partly because I was dying to get away from his commanding gaze, but also because my face was flaming at the thought of Max and his needs.

Jesus, what kind of nanny pictured her boss naked?

A horny one, my inner devil shot back.

I shoved a bite of steak in my mouth and chewed, forcing myself to think of anything but the man across from me.

Desperate for escape and some space between me and Max, the second Dylan was settled and my food was done, I stood from the table and brushed my hands against my jeans.

"All right, well, it's nearly six, so . . ."

I glanced around. I'd already done the cleaning earlier that day, so all that was left was the dinner dishes. Which meant I was done for the day, with nothing left to do.

"Yes, by all means. Go relax," Max said, encouraging me with a smile.

I started for the stairs, then decided a bath and pajamas might be a nice idea—just the thing to put me in a mood for chilling.

I filled the tub and stepped in, luxuriating in the bubbles, and trusted that Max had everything covered. I spent the next hour talking myself down. Max was my boss, and hiding in my room every night after six p.m. like an eighty-five-year-old cat lady was so not going to work for me. I needed to bite the bullet, face my demons—in this case, the luscious Max—and get past this ridiculous schoolgirl crush. The only way around this thing was through it.

When I was done with my bath, I tossed my hair up in a bun, dressed in my pajamas, and headed back down the stairs, filled with a renewed sense of determination. Once I got to know Max and we became friends, I'd see him as more than just the hunky, underwear-model-worthy man of the house. Maybe we could open a bottle of wine and talk. Break the ice. I might even get the chance to ask him about Dylan's mother.

When I arrived in the kitchen, though, it was to find Max poised at the sink, my ceramic coffee mug in his hands.

A surge of guilt rolled over me. He probably hadn't gotten the chance to breathe since he'd walked through the door, and here I was letting him take dish duty while I goofed off.

Noticing my entrance, he turned to face me, and I could have sworn that his gaze raked over me. I crossed my arms over my chest, if only for good measure. I knew the flannel of my pajamas would hide the fact that I wasn't wearing a bra, but with the X-ray heat of his vision, I felt like I couldn't be too sure.

"Where's Dylan?" I asked.

"Asleep. She went out like a light."

I nodded. "Good. She only napped for a half hour that second time, so she was probably pooped." I glanced at the dishes again. "Look, don't you want a couple minutes to yourself? I'm sure I can handle the rest of the dishes."

He looked down at the few plates that were still in the sink. "Are you sure?"

"Absolutely."

"You know, a shower wouldn't be half bad." He turned the water off, then thanked me and left the room.

The dishes were just as quick and easy to finish as expected. I was done within ten minutes, which left me just enough time to scavenge for the bottle of wine I'd picked up at the store. Opening it, I poured two glasses, then stood back and wondered if I was being too forward. What if he didn't like wine? Or what if he didn't want to spend his evening rehashing his past with his daughter's nanny? Or what if—

"Hey."

I turned to find him standing in the doorway wearing nothing but a fitted white T-shirt and jeans. He was frigging sex on legs, and my belly gave a nervous flip, the familiar sense of intimidation and longing mingling in my gut.

Remember the plan. Wine, chat, and get to know him, my inner voice reminded me.

But something told me this was going to be a lot trickier than I'd thought.

Chapter Seven

Max

The half-filled wineglass was a welcome sight. So was Addison, though I hated myself for thinking it. Why the hell hadn't I drawn up some kind of contingency plan for when we were alone together? Maybe developed some kind of new hobby that took me out of the house in the evenings? Or admitted that I was, in fact, Batman and would be super busy fighting crime.

As it was, I hadn't. And here we were. And I was screwed.

"That for me?" I asked.

She nodded. "Yeah, it's a cab. But I can make coffee if you'd rather—"

I shook my head. "No, wine sounds great. I've had a long day, and I wouldn't mind unwinding a little."

She smiled, her full lips curving in the most inviting way. "I know what you mean."

I led her out to the living room, and though she seemed uncertain at first, she followed, settling in beside me on the couch.

Close.

Too fucking close.

I could smell her shampoo, and that alone was making my blood run hot.

"God, I don't know how you drink red wine on here, let alone have a baby crawling around it. I'm getting hives just thinking about spilling." She lifted her glass and I tried to keep my face impassive.

I hadn't even thought about the fact that the furniture would be something of a giveaway. No parent in their right mind would have a white couch with a toddler. Even if I'd thought of it, though, I hadn't had time to replace it. I hadn't had time to do much of anything. One day things were normal, and the next, Dylan was here.

Now, as I pictured those round cheeks and gummy grin, I found it hard to remember exactly what normal was, though.

"Not to mention the white carpet in Dylan's room," Addison added.

"I'm asking for trouble," I said with a nod. I still

wasn't sure how close to keep my cards to my chest, and I hedged, wondering if I should just tell her the whole sordid tale and get it over with. Luckily, she saved me the trouble of having to make my choice just yet.

"You know, I was thinking . . ." She chewed on her bottom lip, and I tried not to stare at the luscious pink curve. "The rest of the house feels so homey and lived-in. Maybe we could spruce up Dylan's room a little too? I mean, I don't know what your budget would be—"

"That sounds like a great idea." I sipped my wine. "Do whatever you want."

"You don't want to have some say in it?" she asked with a frown. "It is your child's room, and I don't want to impose."

I furrowed my brow and shrugged. "Honestly, I wouldn't even know where to start. So have at it."

She laughed, a clear, ringing sound that skimmed along my skin and made my posture relax a little more. "Well, why don't we experiment a little?"

I stared at her, forcing the filthy thoughts of all the ways I'd love to experiment on her from my mind as I waited for her to continue.

"We could both design a room for her, maybe. Have you ever been on Pinterest?" she asked.

This time it was my turn to laugh. "Yeah . . . no. That's the site where women put pictures of coffee cans that they made into flower pots or something, right?"

"Sometimes." She lifted the laptop from the coffee table in front of us and handed it to me. "Here, I have it on my phone, and you can use the one on my laptop. So basically, it's just like an image search. You look around for fun ideas and make a board for them. I'll even make yours for you." She leaned across me, brushing her chest against my arm as she moved. Her hair fell in front of her face, and the lavender smell of her shampoo took hold of me again, sending a rush of blood pulsing to my cock.

I shifted, leaning forward to take another sip of my wine, thanking the gods that her computer was hiding my lap from view.

"There." She looked up at me. "Now enter some search terms like 'cute baby room ideas,' and then use the little red push pins to add things to the board. It will give me an idea of the type of stuff you like. I'll do one too, and in a few minutes, we'll compare and see what we come up with. Ready?"

I nodded, then racked my brain, thinking of what would go best in Dylan's room. I wanted it to be nice— not too frilly, and definitely not all decked out in pink decor and crystal chandeliers. Something she could grow into and enjoy.

I picked my pins carefully, and by the time Addison announced the time was up, I was feeling pretty damn confident about my choices.

"All right, who goes first?" she asked.

"I've got nothing to hide." I shrugged and turned the screen toward her.

She glanced at it, then at me, then at the computer again.

"A big-screen TV? She's one, Max. Plus, you only have three pins," she said. "We've been looking for like twenty minutes."

"The TV is for when she gets older. Or if she wants to watch Barney or something. The dude kind of freaks me out, to be honest, but hey. Kids like him."

She raised her eyebrows. "And the Bob Dylan poster?"

At that, I paused, weighing my options. This was the can of worms that I still hadn't decided if I wanted to open.

"The baby's namesake."

Addison's eyes softened, and she lowered her phone to her lap. "That's really sweet."

Silence filled the air, heavy and pronounced, and when she opened her mouth again, her gaze was thoughtful.

"I know it's not my business. That said, I had wondered . . . if something were to ever happen to you, I know I have your parents' numbers, but—"

She broke off, but I knew the words she would say before she said them.

"What happened to Dylan's mom? I don't want to pry, but I wasn't sure if I could expect her to stop by, or what to say as Dylan grows older and someone asks," she said, looking apologetic.

I let out a sigh. Of course Addison would wonder

that. It was only natural. But how could I tell her the truth? Then again, what choice did I have now?

"Dylan is new to my life, actually," I said, wondering how best to explain what had happened to Jenn—what had happened to me. "I dated her mother, Jenn, for a couple of months last year. I wasn't ready for anything serious and she was, so I broke things off. I didn't hear from her once it ended. Fast forward to a few days ago when she left Dylan on my doorstep and said she couldn't handle it anymore. I had no idea she was ever pregnant."

"Oh my God." Addison raised a hand to her mouth, but before she got the chance to respond, I rushed on.

"Look, I know it's weird. But just because I've only known Dylan for five days doesn't mean that I don't love her as deeply as any father loves his daughter." I didn't know why, but it felt important that Addison knew that. The defensive tone to my voice was hard to hide. Since she'd arrived, there hadn't been a single moment that felt like a sacrifice. Making room for Dylan in my life was easy—I really did love the little thing already.

"This just . . ." She shook her head. "It explains so much."

"It does?"

"There are no pictures of her or Dylan as an infant anywhere. And I couldn't understand why you'd give a baby an entire piece of burned toast with peanut butter on it for breakfast."

I let out a grudging laugh. "I'm clearly still getting a handle on this whole thing."

"So, what happened to Dylan's mother? Where did she go? Does she want to see Dylan again?"

I swallowed. I didn't know the answers to those questions. How could I explain this to Addison if I couldn't even explain it to myself? I'd been the one to screw things up with Jenn in the first place. Maybe if I had just stopped her from leaving, or if I'd told her something, anything, when she'd asked about having a family, I wouldn't have missed the first year of Dylan's life.

I didn't know what she looked like when she was born, and hadn't gotten to celebrate her first steps or her first tooth. It was all my fault. Because Jenn had known she was pregnant when she'd asked about having kids. Instead of probing or realizing how emotional that conversation had been on her part, I'd just written it off and let her go.

These last few days, late at night when I was alone in bed, I'd begun wondering if somewhere deep down, I'd known all along and it had just been more convenient to ignore.

My heart flipped in my chest as I thought of the ramifications of those actions.

Jesus, what if Jenn hadn't brought her to me? What if I'd missed countless more milestones as Dylan grew up without her father?

I cleared my tightening throat and shrugged, turning my attention back to Addison, who waited patiently for my reply.

"I'm not sure what Jenn's plans are, but no matter what, Dylan will be in my life going forward," I said finally.

Addison nodded. "She's a lucky girl."

I winced and took another slug of wine. "Debatable."

She patted my arm gently and then pulled her hand away. "I see how you are with her. You're a natural when it comes to the important stuff, like love and attention.

And hey, we've all got our regrets, you know?"

"Do we?"

She pursed her lips, apparently at war with herself, then in a too-casual tone, she said, "Sure. Hey, I turned my last boyfriend gay, so . . . you know, sometimes life is full of curveballs."

"You did not turn him gay," I scoffed.

"I promise you, he was definitely gay, and you do not want to know the details."

"That's not what I mean," I said. "You didn't *turn* him gay. He probably just wasn't willing to admit to himself or anybody else that he was gay, and you got caught in the crosshairs. Happens to more people than you think."

She rolled her eyes and took another sip of her wine.

"Truly, any man would be lucky to have you. You're beautiful and funny and smart."

She looked up at me through her thick lashes, a soft, thoughtful expression in her eyes. A pretty pink blush colored her cheeks as she said, "Thank you."

I shook my head, ignoring the pulse fluttering in her neck and the swell of her breasts. "Just stating the facts. Now, you still have to show me what you came up with that is apparently so much better than a sweet-ass baby cave with a big-screen TV and a Dylan poster."

"Oh, you're on!"

She clicked on her phone, then handed it to me. It looked like a real little girl's room—pictures of boxy white bookcases filled with brightly colored books, stuffed animals, and toys abounded. There were soft, fluffy blankets, and in one picture, just above the crib, hung a hand-painted plaque with the quote, "She be small but mighty."

Everything was in shades of dove gray and pink with touches of yellow. These were only pictures, but I already felt like it was special somehow. Like it had all been put together just for Dylan.

"This is great," I said sincerely. "I'm impressed."

Addison shrugged, and her fingers brushed over mine as she reclaimed her phone. "One of my favorite hobbies. It's nothing."

"I beg to differ."

She rolled her eyes again.

"Are you always so hard on yourself?" I asked.

Her blush deepened, and she swirled her wine thoughtfully. "Maybe. It's just ... you wouldn't understand."

"Try me," I said, and something in my tone made her straighten. She let out a deep breath, her brow furrowing again.

"Fine. It's just like, have you ever felt like a complete disaster area?"

I nodded. "When I first started my construction business, I knew I was going to torch everything important to me. I'd left the Army and the promise of a promotion to do something I had no experience in. It's just one of those things you have to let play out. I love working with my hands, and if I hadn't given it a try—"

She shook her head furiously. "No, it's like ever since everything happened with Greg, I feel like I'm a failure, you know? I'm a disappointment." Her face turned the brightest shade of red yet as she mumbled, "In the guy department. Ugh, this might be the wine talking, but I feel like he shattered my confidence. Like no man will ever truly want me."

"If we'd met under different circumstances, I would show you how very wrong you are." The words came out before I could stop them and in a voice that had dropped to a low growl.

Addison stared at me, her mouth half-open, her eyes unblinking.

What the fuck was wrong with me?

Sure, I was attracted to her, more than attracted. If she were anyone else, I would have been unbuttoning her pajama top an hour ago. Hell, I might have fucked her right on the kitchen table if she was down.

But she *wasn't* anyone else. She was Dylan's nanny. And a great one at that.

I could be attracted to her, but I had to keep my dick in my pants—especially now that I was rock hard, thinking about her spreading her legs open for me on the kitchen table.

I cleared my throat and slapped my hands on my

knees. Time to retreat before I fucked this up even harder.

"Anyway, I better get to bed. Big day tomorrow."

"Um, yeah, g'night," she murmured, her words barely above a whisper.

I left my wineglass on the table and stood, careful to hide my erection as I marched up the stairs and disappeared into my bathroom.

"Dammit," I muttered under my breath.

Total clusterfuck. She could be down there right now wondering if she should pack her bags and bolt.

Then I thought back to her expression at the end there. The way her pupils had dilated, the way her delicate nostrils had flared, just slightly. Had her nipples gone hard beneath that pajama top?

I groaned again and slid my hand down the front of my straining zipper. No way I was going to get any rest tonight until I tamed this fucking beast. I took my cock in hand, thinking of how soft and supple Addison's skin would be against my chest. The lavender smell of her hair. The heat in her eyes when I'd all but told her how much I wanted her.

I gripped myself harder, imagining that it was her full lips wrapped around my cock instead, working me up and down while her tongue lapped at the head, teasing me before she dipped lower and took all of me into her mouth.

Damn, how I'd like to weave my fingers through her hair and feel her tits brush against my thighs while she was on her knees in front of me, sucking every last inch and still moaning for more.

She didn't feel sexy or desirable? By the time I was finished with her, she would feel like a fucking goddess. The way she walked, the way she moved her hips, I knew that she would be heaven between the sheets.

Or on top of a table.

Or against the wall.

Or in the fucking street, for all I cared.

I imagined myself sinking between her thighs and pushing deep, feeling her hips grind against me while I worked her sweet pink pussy.

Fuck, if she let me at her, she would have all the confidence in the world.

My balls drew up and I suppressed a groan as the need to come filled me. Working myself harder and faster, I closed my eyes, imagining those sweet lips wrapped around me, those wide eyes staring into mine.

"Fu-uck!"

I came in a hot, pulsing surge, relishing the wave of euphoria that swept over me, making my muscles quake. My breath was coming in long drags as I let my eyes slip open again.

No big deal. This was perfectly normal for a red-blooded male living with sex on a stick. The old nanny fantasy.

In my dirty mind, Addison was the perfect sensual vixen, ripe for the taking.

And in my mind was exactly where she'd have to stay.

Chapter Eight

Addison

Light streamed into the room and I blinked, rolling over to grab my phone from the nightstand beside me. Clicking it on, I glanced at the time and gasped.

"Shit." I jumped from the bed and rushed to the baby's room, my hands already outstretched to soothe whatever tears were surely waiting for me.

Why had the baby monitor stopped working? And why hadn't Max woken me up before he left? He was already long gone—had probably left an hour ago, which meant Dylan was completely unattended and it was entirely my fault. If she was hurt or hungry . . .

I pushed open the door to find Dylan standing at the bars of her crib, gurgling happily, and I let out a sigh of relief.

"Thank God," I breathed, moving closer to scoop her into my arms. As I approached, I noticed something else—a little piece of paper, the same shade of white as the crib, with tiny, scrawled words in cramped lettering.

Addison—

Sorry I missed you. The baby got up at the crack of dawn so we had a daddy/daughter early morning. She's fed and changed and needed a few more Zs, so I figured I'd let her wake you when she was ready.

Have a great day,

Max

I blinked. "Have a great day?" That was it?

Why the hell would he get up so early with the baby when he had to work all day? Unless . . .

I scrubbed my free hand over my face and then lifted Dylan from her crib.

I'd overstepped last night—gotten too personal too fast. And now, of course, he was avoiding me.

Greg had done that too. When I'd first confronted him about his proclivities in the bedroom, he'd shied away from me and barely spoken to me for a week. He'd told me that I ran over him like a steamroller, that I didn't give him time to express himself naturally.

Had I done that to Max too?

Dylan strained to get down and I set her gently onto the carpet. She toddled toward the little box full of toys I'd brought for her yesterday, and I glanced around the room.

This place alone should have been clue enough that Dylan hadn't been living here long. Aside from the barely stocked white changing table and the matching white crib, the room was bare. The walls were white and the windows were undressed. It was more fitting for a nunnery than a nursery.

"We're going to have to do something about this, little lady," I told Dylan.

"Ball," she responded, holding one up to show me.

"Smart little girl."

I pulled her into my arms again and carried her downstairs, careful to make sure her ball was in tow, and together we started our daily routine. We made breakfast together and ate, and afterward, I built a fort for her with the spare linens in the hall closet.

Like I had the day before, I texted pictures and

messages to Max, and little gray checks appeared on my screen, letting me know he'd seen my messages and had chosen not to respond.

Well, that was okay. After all, he hadn't responded yesterday either.

Still, I couldn't shake the mental image of him grimacing when he saw my name flash on his phone screen. Like just looking at what I said—no matter what it was—was some colossal reminder of what an oversharing, prying asshole I was. And then I'd gone and made it a billion times worse by telling him the story about Greg. Max had probably felt obligated to make me feel better, hence his panty-melting declaration, but that didn't change the fact that I'd overstepped.

There was nothing to do about that now, so Dylan and I went on with our day, playing and cleaning and laughing until the doorbell rang at three in the afternoon.

I frowned, wondering if Max might be expecting a package, but when I made it to the door, I found a tall, leggy woman grinning at me. She was in a gray business suit that perfectly matched the color of her eyes and set off the bright red of her hair.

I sucked in my cheeks, uncomfortably aware of the fact that Dylan and I had deemed today a pajama day.

"Hello," I said. "How can I help you?"

"Oh, hi." Her voice was just as chipper as her smile, but something about it sounded too shrill and wrong—almost like she'd had to rehearse what it sounded like to be polite. She took a step inside the house and I backed away, somewhat at a loss as she stuck her hand out toward me.

I accepted it and shook it, not sure what else to do.

"I'm Tiffany, Max's assistant. I was in the area, and Max asked me to drop by and let you know he'd be working late tonight. He also wanted me to see if you all were doing all right?" She glanced over at the linen fort, which was primarily held up by the vacuum Dylan had taken to sitting on like it was a pony.

"There's the little angel," she cooed, striding past me and making a beeline toward Dylan.

The baby's eyes widened and she scrambled from her seat, retreating deeper into the fort.

"Sorry," I said. "Almost nap time. She's a little

fussy."

"Quite all right." Tiffany sank onto her knees and started slapping her lap like she was inviting a puppy to play fetch. "Come here, Dylan. Come say hello."

Dylan didn't move, and I cleared my throat.

"So," Tiffany said as she twisted to look at me. "You guys are getting along all right?"

"Very well, thank you." I tried hard not to grit my teeth, but this bitch was getting on my nerves now. What was I, some high-school babysitter who needed checking up on? I was a professional. Why the hell would he have this woman march in here and interrupt our routine like this without telling me she was coming?

Exactly right.

Whatever Max's reasons, it wasn't his assistant's fault.

I blew out a sigh, irrationally feeling hurt. Then I knelt onto the floor beside her and motioned for Dylan to come toward me. When she did, I gestured to Tiffany.

"Dylan, will you say hello to Tiffany?" I asked.

The baby waved a chubby fist and Tiffany caught it

eagerly, shaking it like they'd just made a business deal on *Shark Tank*.

"So nice to see you again, little miss," Tiffany cooed.

"Oh, you've met before?" My eyebrows inched higher. Max had said Dylan had only been here a few days before I'd been hired. But then, that would have been over the weekend, so ... "Did Max bring her into the office?"

Jealousy? This was new.

"Oh yes, but we met before that too. Dylan and I go way back." She winked at the baby. "I can never get over how cute she is. Such beautiful eyes, just like her father." Her tone suggested she'd seen a lot more than Max's eyes, and I struggled to remain impassive.

"She certainly does," I said, and Dylan scooted off my lap and crawled back into the sanctuary of her fort.

"I can't imagine what it's like to live with him," Tiffany went on, apparently not sensing what I thought was my very obvious discomfort with the subject.

"Oh, so far it's been easy. Maybe he's just got his best foot forward. Should I be worried? Does he leave the seat up or is it something worse?" I said with a forced grin.

"No, no, no. He's just an exacting kind of man, you know? A lot of successful businessmen like him are. Plus the military training. His housekeeper must have almost nothing to do."

I remained silent, not wanting to divulge the utter chaos I'd walked into the day before, slightly mollified that Miss Tiffany didn't know as much as she thought she did. "Yes, he mentioned the Army."

"Yup, he was a Ranger. Quite the accomplishment." She said this as though she had given him the title herself.

"Oh, how interesting. You'd never know it," I said.

"Unless you look at his tattoos. But you probably haven't seen the one on his back," Tiffany said with a wink, and I feigned a smile in return.

"Right. Well, I do appreciate you stopping by and checking on us. We're going to get ready for naptime, but you can let him know that we're all just fine here. I hope he doesn't have to work too long."

Tiffany sighed. "A workaholic. Another fault, I'm

afraid. But yes, I'll tell him you're good. You're sure you don't need anything at all?"

I glanced at Dylan and tilted my mouth to the side. In truth, I'd been hoping to talk to him about the nursery over dinner, but if he wasn't coming home . . .

"Well, we had talked about me sprucing up the baby's room a little. Can you have him call me about that?"

Tiffany cut in with a tight laugh. "Oh, you should definitely go. Do you need a credit card?" She rifled inside her big red bag and pulled out a gold credit card.

"Uh, thanks," I said, taking the card.

"And I agree with you that room could use some work. Make sure you sneak in a couple of dollies and maybe a tiara for the little princess too," she whispered with a wink.

I thanked her and showed her to the door. Then, when I heard her car door shut, I joined Dylan in her fort and kissed her forehead.

Max could have sent me a message. He could have left it in his note before he'd left for work.

But no, he'd sent that woman here to check on me. A sliver of annoyance curled itself around my growing self-doubt, and I scooped up the baby and carried her upstairs.

"Come on, Dylan. After your nap, we're going to the hit the town for some retail therapy."

Chapter Nine

Max

When I pulled up to the house, Addison's sporty red Maxima was gone and there were no lights shining through the windows.

I checked my phone, thinking maybe I'd missed a message, but the screen held no notifications except for a reminder that Tiffany had sent for a meeting next week.

Quickly, I dialed Addison and stepped inside the house, calling out for her and Dylan a few times before I finally made my way up to the nursery. It was empty and dark, just like everywhere else.

I called her phone again. And then a third time, still with no answer.

"It's probably fine," I mumbled under my breath, but it didn't stop my heart from pounding. My blood thundered in my ears as I scrolled through my contacts again, stopping when I reached Tiffany's number.

I dialed her, listening to the agonizing ring, and then it clicked to life.

"Hey there," she said.

"Hey, this is a weird question, but Addison didn't call you, did she?" I asked.

There was a pause. "Addison? Your nanny?"

"Yeah."

"No. Why? What's going on?" Tiffany asked. There was a clatter of noise in the background, and I felt guilty for interrupting whatever she was doing, but I pressed on.

"I just came home and nobody's here. I didn't know if she might have left a message with you at the office and you forgot to tell me."

"Do you want me to come over and keep you company? Maybe try to help call around?" she asked.

"No, I've already interrupted you enough. Thanks, anyway."

"Keep me posted," she said.

I turned off the phone and stared down at it, wondering what my next move was. It was too early to call the police—and if Addison and Dylan had only run up the street for something, I'd feel like a jackass. Still, it didn't seem like Addison not to message me.

I opened her messages from earlier in the day, reviewing the picture of Dylan covered in applesauce, and another of the blanket fort they'd made, but none of the messages hinted that they were heading out later.

Why wouldn't Addison have told me where she was going? Surely, she knew that I'd be worried.

Maybe she'd called my mother? Or my father? I scrolled to their numbers, my thumb hovering over DIAL when headlights shone through the front bay windows.

I stepped onto the porch, my pulse still hammering, to see Addison pulling Dylan from her car seat, her free hand laden with bags of all different colors and sizes.

"Let me help."

Addison shot me a strained smile. "Thanks."

I rushed over, took Dylan from her, and scooped up some bags, embarrassed by the rush of relief I felt when the baby was finally in my arms again. She snuggled close, burying her face into my neck. Everything was all right. Dylan was fine, and Addison was fine. All was right with the world.

So then why was my stomach still churning?

Afraid to speak for fear of what might come out of my mouth, I turned and carried Dylan inside and set the bags down, then took her up to her room. After quickly changing her into her footie pajamas, I settled her in her crib. She was clearly exhausted because she lay down without complaint. I read her a book and within minutes, her eyelids drooped and closed.

For a long moment, I stood by her crib and stared at her. Parenthood was a real motherfucker sometimes. There had been no sign of a struggle. No ransom note or reason for panic. But my hands were still clammy with icy fear, and my fury was mounting.

I knew Addison cared for Dylan, but who did she think she was, leaving the house without a note or even a quick text to let me know they wouldn't be here when I got home? I still couldn't shake the knot in my gut, and there was only one person to blame.

I could hear Addison bustling around downstairs, and I balled my fists at my sides and took the stairs two at a time to find her standing in the middle of the living room, pulling items from the multicolored bags.

"Where the hell were you?" I hadn't made it all the way down the steps yet, and for a second I worried the volume and harshness of my tone would wake the baby.

Addison blinked up at me with wide, confused eyes. "What do you mean?"

"I mean, where the hell were you? It's eight o'clock. That's past Dylan's bedtime. I get home and find an empty house. No message, no note. What the hell was I supposed to think?"

"W-we went shopping," she stuttered. "I went to get things for the baby's room like we talked about last night, but then it was late and Dylan was hungry, so we went on a dinner date. I didn't expect to be gone for so long."

My heart softened a little at the idea of the two of them sitting at dinner together, enjoying themselves, but that did nothing to dissolve the memory of the very real terror and dread she'd left me to face.

"I didn't know you'd be going today."

"I mentioned it to Tiffany when she stopped by earlier. I thought she'd tell you once she got back to the office."

I opened my mouth again, debating what to say next, but Addison ducked her head and skirted past me, back out the front door. She left it open behind her, and I stared into space until she reappeared with yet another bag in her hand.

"I don't know if you like Italian, but I ordered something for you and had them pack it up just in case you hadn't had dinner. It's probably still warm."

I took the bag and looked inside to find spaghetti and meatballs in a clear container, waiting for me.

"I hope you don't mind, but there's a little bite taken out of one of your meatballs. Dylan was curious." Addison chewed on her bottom lip, and my tense muscles loosened.

It was thoughtful of her to have gotten this for me, even if she'd been careless about keeping me informed. It was a gesture she hadn't had to make, but she'd done it anyway. And her bond with Dylan was so clear to see already. That was the important thing. Forgetting to tell me her plans had been an honest mistake, and one I was sure she wouldn't repeat.

"Make sure to send me a text if you're going to leave

next time, okay?" I let out a little sigh, then walked over to examine what she'd picked out for Dylan's room. It was like her Pinterest board come to life—stacks of books, and a box with a light gray bookcase inside. And a framed Bob Dylan album too.

It must have taken her hours to find it all, and my overreaction seemed all the more stark to me. *Nice job, dickhead.*

"I'm sorry for freaking out," I said as I looked over everything. "This is all new to me, and to be honest, it scared the shit out of me."

"Don't worry about it." She rounded the couch to join me. "I should probably apologize too, actually. I've been thinking about it, and I'm pretty embarrassed about the way I behaved yesterday. I shouldn't have told you all that stuff about me and Greg. I'm imagining that was why you decided to work late, and why I felt so compelled to get out of the house and all. Then I was too embarrassed to call you. It was just the start of a weird vibe, and I shouldn't have said any of it."

I waved her off. "The only thing you have to be sorry about is that you wasted your time with that jackass to begin with. I stand by what I said. Any man would be lucky to have you."

Instantly, I regretted the nicety. It was like all the air had been sucked from the room, and all that remained was the reminder of what I'd said to her last night, and the mutual understanding that I could never prove what I'd said.

She glanced away, a chocolate-brown lock falling in front of her face. I itched to reach out and tuck it behind her ear, to pull her face closer until she was only inches from me, and then . . . But that was a slippery slope, and I was already skating a little too close to the edge.

"Did you have a good day at least?" I asked, and she looked back at me, thoughtful for a moment.

"Yes, mostly. It was a little odd, though."

"Crazy at the mall?"

She shook her head. "No, not that."

"Well, don't keep me in suspense."

She blew out a sigh and shrugged. "I'm not sure exactly what I did wrong. I definitely would've texted, but Tiffany told me you were going to be home really late when she stopped by this afternoon, so I didn't even think you'd be aware we were gone, never mind worried about Dylan. And Tiffany knew that I was going to take the baby to the mall because she offered me your credit card to use, so I'd assumed you'd authorized that."

"Tiffany was here?" I asked. Why the hell hadn't she mentioned that? I thought back to the conversation. Why did she act like she had no clue where they might be? Unless Tiffany had just assumed that their outing would be a daytime one, and so she was truly at a loss about where they'd be tonight.

"Yeah." Addison nodded. Her lips quirked a little. "It was a little odd. She gave off a certain kind of vibe."

"What kind of vibe?" I asked.

Addison blushed to the roots of her hair. "I don't want to throw anyone under the bus."

"This is important, Addison."

"Fine." She let out a sigh. "She sort of admitted that she knew you . . . very well. I got the impression that you and she were a bit of an item."

"Ah." My mouth went dry and I thought about

pulling my phone from my pocket and dialing Tiffany right on the spot. But all I said was, "We're not."

"I see." Addison glanced away again, apparently intent on something in the corner of the room.

"We were . . . sort of. At one time. We had a close call once, but I stopped things before they went too far. If she still has feelings for me, they certainly aren't reciprocated, and I'll talk to her about this."

"Oh, please, I don't want to cause any trouble." Addison held up her hands in front of her like she was trying to catch a soccer ball. "I just didn't want you to think that I would be careless with Dylan's safety like that. I'll text you directly next time."

I frowned. "I know better than to think you would be careless with anything. I jumped to conclusions out of fear."

Again, the pounding silence filled my ears and my breath caught as I waited for Addison to say something else, to take the stillness and anticipation from the air.

"That's very nice of you to say," she said softly.

"I mean it. You're a great nanny. Not a second has

gone by when I regretted my choice in hiring you."

Except, of course, all the times I wanted to bend you over the kitchen counter and make you scream my name.

Apparently, I wasn't the only one thinking of the exception either, because Addison asked, "Even with what you said the other night? About . . ." She cleared her throat. "If you hadn't hired me? Did you mean that?"

"Of course I meant it. You're smart and beautiful and nurturing. You're . . ." I caught myself and stopped, noticing the glow in her eyes and the sudden tightening in my pants. *Shit.* "I meant it," I finished.

"That means a lot to me too." She swallowed. "Really. Not that it matters."

"Why not?" I asked, struck by the rosiness of her cheeks. I wanted to run my finger along the curve of her jaw, to touch her skin to see if it was as warm as it looked.

"Because you *did* hire me. Obviously," she said, softer still.

"Obviously." I nodded.

A long pause passed between us as electricity snapped and spun in the air. I was inches from her, and all

I had to say was that we shouldn't let that stop us—that I wanted her no matter what.

But then a wail sounded from upstairs, and Addison shot to her feet.

"Dylan. She probably needs changing." She rushed toward the stairs.

"Let me take care of it," I said, but she shook her head.

"No, no. You eat. I've got it. Promise," she said and disappeared up the stairs.

I glanced at my food, still sitting on the coffee table. The moment of heavy, hot tension was gone.

And frankly? I wasn't sure if I was disappointed or relieved.

Chapter Ten

Addison

It was official. I'd gotten through my first week as Dylan's nanny, and I'd only embarrassed myself marginally.

Okay, a lot.

Still, I could manage a little mortification if it let me keep this job for as long as possible. Dylan was an absolute dream, and the more time I spent with her, the more I fell head over heels in love. Whenever she smiled, I found myself smiling back, and when she laughed, my heart flipped over in my chest.

As for Max? Well, he'd been nice enough about my many snafus, and there was no doubt that our relationship was changing too. Unlike with Dylan, Max and I were capable of carrying on a conversation, and the general awkwardness of my first few days had gently begun to fade, giving way to more natural conversation. Over dinner a few days ago, he'd shared with me the story of his Army Ranger training. I'd asked him why he'd chosen the military, and he looked at me thoughtfully for a moment.

"It's a family thing. My grandfather was in the Army, and my father was a Ranger too. He went the more traditional path, but when I left the military, I think he understood."

"What do you mean?" I'd asked.

"Well, by the time my last tour was up, my father had retired here, and my whole family had settled down in this town. My dad always had a sort of knack for adventure, but I was always more drawn to stability. He wanted to go and jet set, and I wanted to build a life and a home." Max shook his head. "Don't get me wrong, my work as a Ranger was important, but what I do now, getting my hands dirty and building new things? That's what I really love."

I'd thought about that conversation for the rest of the night, wondering what exactly he meant by wanting stability and a home. If he hadn't been with Dylan's mother long, was it because she wasn't the right woman or was it because he flitted from girl to girl? If he wanted a place to lay his head down at night, did that mean he was looking for commitment and love and all that?

I didn't know, but I also couldn't avoid the fact that

it was none of my business either way.

But he was attracted to me . . .

Every day since he'd called me beautiful and told me that he wanted me, I couldn't keep it from my mind. When I handed him his coffee in the morning, it was the first thing I wanted to say, almost like a child who wanted validation. I'd turn around and think, *Do you still want me today? Do you still want to show me what it's like to be a woman?*

Every time, it made my cheeks heat and my palms sweat, but I couldn't drive it out of my mind. And as if that weren't enough to handle, I could tell his unspoken answer by the way he looked at me.

It was hard to describe, really. I'd had men look at me with interest before, but this was completely different. Sometimes, it was as though he could see me, all naked and raw in front of him, and other times it was as though he could see even further than that—into my soul.

I'd been on the point of saying it to him too. Like one night, when he'd put Dylan to sleep and I'd put on some brainless Netflix show just to have something to look at. It had been a long day and Dylan had been fussier than usual, but once Max sat down next to me and offered me a glass of wine, it was like my nerves were quelled and charged all at once.

"Who were you on the phone with?" he'd asked.

I blinked, remembering the phone call I'd taken while making dinner.

"Oh, my friend Lara. She wants to hang out this weekend."

"You can invite her over, you know. This is your house too."

I shook my head. "No, no, it's fine. You and Dylan deserve some time alone without me in your hair."

"You know, at first I thought you were talking to your mother."

I laughed. "Lara would love that. Her greatest joy is bossing me around. No, my mom doesn't pick up the phone much. She works for the CDC, and it keeps her pretty busy."

"That's gotta be tough, not hearing from her." His eyes softened, and I blanched.

"It's okay. I've got other things." I looked at the TV,

trying to focus on the show, but I knew his eyes were still on me, surveying me. I felt like he could read my mind, could feel my memories, and if I was honest, my hurt. With each conversation, I was feeling closer to him and more torn up inside about it.

But I couldn't focus on all that. I had a good thing here, and I wasn't about to blow it over a crush.

Why, oh why does it feel like so much more than a crush?

Some time away from Max was exactly what the doctor ordered so I could get my head on straight again. Lara would help me clear my head.

With a sigh, I looked around Dylan's newly finished room. I'd painted a few stencils on the walls and set up all the new furniture. Beside her rocking chair was a record player with the Bob Dylan album hanging above it. Sometimes I'd play her a song in the middle of the day and rock her there. Other times, I sat in the chair and watched her paw through her brand-new toy chest. I had to admit, I'd done good with the room.

My hands on my hips, I nodded to myself and then headed down to the already bustling kitchen.

When I walked through the archway, I found Dylan in her high chair, halfway through demolishing her pile of pancake bits, and Max in a chair in front of her. He turned to face me, and his eyes sparked with something I couldn't name.

Desire, maybe? I pushed the thought away.

"Dylan's room is finally finished, and I'm going to head out."

"Already? You can't make us pancakes and then not have any yourself," Max argued. "There's still coffee too."

"It's okay. I've got an hour's drive ahead of me, so I want to get on the road."

"At least take some coffee with you in a thermos." He motioned to the pot, but I shook my head.

"If you're on your own with her all day, you might need that," I said.

"You're probably right." He stood from his seat and walked toward me. Slowly, the clean, fresh scent of him took over my senses, and I held my breath to keep from getting dragged into the storm of wanting him. When he was only inches from me, I stiffened.

"Sorry, I just wanna get to the coffeepot," he murmured.

I glanced beside me to see the pot and let out a little sigh of relief mixed with regret. "Oh, right."

"Look, I know I've already said it, but thank you so much for taking care of Dylan's room like that. I really appreciate it. I couldn't have done it without you."

His gaze trailed over me, and I felt that all-too-familiar heat creeping up the back of my neck, ready to flood my cheeks.

"No problem at all, really. Well, I better be off."

I kissed Dylan good-bye and waved to Max, then scooped up my bag and rushed to my car.

When I was safe behind the wheel and on my way, I cranked up the radio and rolled down the windows, letting the warm early September air fill my lungs. Without Max around, I finally felt like I could breathe. Use this time to be myself without the eggshells and worries. Some time to reflect.

For the better part of the drive, though, all I could manage to do was reflect on him.

What was his deal? I knew that he was fond of his mother, had done well in school, had been friends with the same group of people for most of his adult life, but the one thing he never mentioned? Women.

Aside from Dylan's mother, there was no hint that he'd ever been with someone, and yet . . . A man like that had to get around, didn't he? Between his rich, dark hair and his deep, dark eyes, women probably threw themselves at him pretty regularly. Did he go along for the ride, or was he a relationship guy?

I didn't know. All I knew was this Max, the one who was new to fatherhood. When things settled down and he'd accepted his role in Dylan's life, would he get back to dating again? And, worse, would he parade these women around the house, right in front of me? Or maybe he would take them to hotels or stay over at their house for the weekend. I'd have to make excuses for him to Dylan, knowing all the while where he was and what—or who— he was doing.

I gripped the wheel tighter, hating the knot that was tying up my stomach.

My interest in Max's dating life was all professional,

of course. His relationships with women were sure to affect Dylan in the long term.

Nice try, loser. Plenty of single parents date.

Besides, if it was all about Dylan, then why did I feel murderous when I thought about him taking another woman into his arms, or worse, his bed?

I agonized over that very thought until I reached the parking lot of the salon where I was scheduled to meet Lara. When I pushed open the doors, a little chime tinkled, and I found her sitting in the waiting area, looking up at me.

"I hate this hour-drive thing," she said with a scowl. "I like you close."

I waved my hand. "Hello to you too."

"Well, obviously hello." She hugged me swiftly, then motioned to one of the girls behind the counter to let them know we were ready. They led us back to a room with a tiny waterfall and a row of chairs with deep, jetted basins for our feet.

"I signed us up for mani-pedis," she explained. "Hope that's okay."

"Perfect." I relaxed into my chair and let out a deep breath.

"Long week?" she asked.

"You know how it is starting a new job."

"And being constantly surrounded by Mr. Hot Bod? Can't say that I do," Lara said, and the woman working on her heel looked over at me.

I smiled at her, then turned back to Lara with gritted teeth. "Please, for the love of God, don't call him that."

"Fine, fine, call him what you want. How is it going with him?"

"With my boss? He's fine. Happy with my performance."

Lara waggled her eyebrows. "Oh, is he now?"

I pinched the bridge of my nose between two fingers. "Do we have to go over this every time we talk?" I'd just spent the whole ride over remembering all the reasons I had to stop thinking about Max, and now Lara seemed determined to drag me back to ground zero again.

"I've just been thinking. You know, it might be fun."

"What?" I asked.

"Getting down and dirty with Mr. Boss Man."

"He has a name," I shot back.

"Max, then. Do you think he might be interested?" Lara asked.

She knew me too well for me to hide my blush, so I looked away. "I'm not talking about this anymore."

"So he *is* interested," she squawked, clapping her hands together gleefully. "Juicy. Do tell."

"There is . . . a sort of mutual attraction. But I told you before, I'm done with guys for now. The last time I got involved, I wound up homeless. I live with this guy too, remember, and I'm sure you don't want me sleeping on your couch again."

"It depends. How many pints of ice cream are you going to buy me?" she asked. "I kind of loved having all those flavors in the freezer at any given time."

I raised an eyebrow. "Lara."

She held up her hands. "Fine, fine, you're probably right. Look, but don't touch."

"Exactly." I nodded.

I should get that tattooed on me, just as a constant reminder.

As the day progressed, though, as much fun as I was having catching up with my bestie, I couldn't help but wonder how Dylan was. If she missed me. If her daddy missed me.

But it was exactly that—the thoughts of Dylan and how much I missed her grinning face—that had me feeling more sure than ever.

Most relationships didn't work out. That was straight statistics. Which meant that even if Max and I dated, we'd likely fail, and then what? I'd lose my job, again, my home, again, and worse? I'd lose Dylan.

It was too big of a risk to take, no matter how sexy Max was.

Look, but don't touch.

My new mantra.

If he could just do the same, we'd be golden.

Chapter Eleven

Max

I rounded my truck and gazed into the bed, wiping a bead of sweat from my face.

"Shit," I murmured. I'd forgotten Zach's favorite beer, and given his reputation for being picky, he wasn't likely to forgive me for it. Quickly, I pulled my phone from my pocket and texted Matt to bring some with him, then loaded the grocery bags and boxes into my arms and made for my front door.

I couldn't deny that a certain amount of guilt was settling in the pit of my stomach—not that it was my fault. I probably should have told Addison that the guys were coming over for the first football game of the season, but I hadn't wanted to bother her while she was with her friend yesterday. Then, by the time I saw her this morning, she was so harried with cleaning and caring for Dylan that it completely slipped my mind.

Now, though, I was going to have to give her a heads-up barely five minutes before the guys were due to walk through the door.

When I got to the kitchen, I called for Dylan and Addison, then settled my bags onto the counter and looked around. The house was quiet, and I was on the brink of heading upstairs to look for them when I heard a shrill laugh through the back window.

Turning on my heel, I headed for the back door and opened it to find Dylan sitting in a little two-piece pink bikini with white polka dots, her chubby belly jiggling with peals of laughter as a sprinkler moved back and forth, spraying water over her head.

Standing above her, trying to convince her to toddle over the sprinkler, was Addison. Who, as it happened, was also wearing a bikini.

And it was nearly as small as Dylan's.

My cock thickened and I swallowed hard, trying to ignore the long, trim length of her legs and the golden skin exposed by her dark blue suit. My eyes must have been bugging out of my head, and I blinked before I heard the front door open behind me.

Shit.

"Hey, where are you?" Matt's voice echoed through

the house as he walked through to the kitchen, swiftly followed by Zach. "I didn't stop. I just told Zach he was going to have to suck it up and drink real beer for a change."

"Just because I like lime in my beer—" Zach started, then he stopped when he found me, still frozen in the doorway.

"I hope you don't mind." Addison grinned at me. "It was such a beautiful day, and I thought we'd soak up the last of the summer sun, you know?"

Heat pricked at the back of my neck, and I was all too aware that Addison was in full view of both Zach and Matt. They could see, just like I could, all the curves and planes of her body.

"Why don't you go put some clothes on?" I asked, my voice curt as I turned back to my friends. "Give me a minute here, guys. Turn on the game in the living room, and I'll be right in."

Zach said, "Fine, I'll drink your disgusting beer, but I swear to God, if we don't have hot wings, somebody is gonna get hit."

"Save it," Matt muttered, and nodded at me before he led Zach back through the kitchen.

Quickly, I crossed the yard and scooped Dylan up from the ground, groaning as her wet swimsuit dampened the front of my shirt.

"I could have done that," Addison said, but I ignored her.

"You could have brought out a towel too," I grumbled under my breath.

Instead, though, she was going to traipse through the living room under my friends' watchful eyes, letting her luscious ass hang out for everyone to see.

This wasn't me. Jealousy, macho asshole anger? Just not my bag, but there was no question my blood ran hot with fury at the thought, and no matter how hard I tried, I couldn't shake it.

Gritting my teeth, I carried Dylan up to her room and dressed her in a pair of pajamas, then carried her right back down and sat her on the carpet in front of the TV. Handing her some plastic keys to play with, I sat back with my friends and tried to focus on the game.

"The place looks different," Matt said.

"Clean," Zach agreed, and I nodded.

"Addison does a lot around the house," I said, then glanced at the steps. She'd probably come back down here at any minute, and when she did, I'd have to introduce her to everyone.

No matter what she changed into, though, I knew my friends would see her as I still did in my mind's eye—all creamy skin and luscious curves. Her bikini top had been too small for her, and her modest cleavage had been enhanced to the point that all I could think about was thrusting my cock in that tight vee and sliding it up and down . . .

I stuffed my hands in my pockets and leaned back into the couch.

"Do she and Dylan play in the sprinklers a lot?" Zach asked, his face the picture of innocence. Dylan turned, gurgling at the sound of her name. "And if so, what times of day? Asking for a friend."

Matt barked out a laugh. "Yeah, I could probably use some cooling off myself."

"That's enough," I snapped, and Zach flipped me the bird before focusing back on the game.

Something was happening on the screen—someone had been fouled or had fouled someone else—but my mind was too busy reeling to keep track. All I could do was think about those damn long legs and how they would feel wrapped around my waist. Her soft brown hair pulled into a high ponytail, and how that ponytail would look bouncing as she sucked my cock.

This was so not going to work.

"Actually, I think I better put Dylan down for a nap," I muttered, then scooped up the baby and hauled her upstairs like I was sprinting for my own touchdown. She babbled a little and I heard my friends cheer from downstairs, but I kissed the top of her head and laid her in the crib all the same.

Damn, I seriously hadn't thought anything through today. It was close to her naptime, but even if she slept, they would wake her in a matter of minutes. Football and babies might not mix. We were going to have to move the Sunday game ritual to a new location.

One that didn't include my boys seeing my smoking-hot nanny in her bathing suit.

As an image of that tight little ass filled my mind again, I groaned, wishing I hadn't seen her either. What the fuck was I going to do about Addison?

I had a few ideas, of course, but most of those involved restraints and scented massage oils.

In the hall, I heard her bedroom door click shut and I waited for a long moment, weighing my options. But how many times could I do this—over and over again and still coming to the same result? It wasn't working. None of this was working.

I marched to her door and knocked hard.

After a slight pause, she called, "Come in."

When I walked inside, she was wearing a fluffy pink robe that stopped just above her knees. Her swimsuit was on the floor in front of her, and my mind was momentarily sidetracked by the fact that I knew she was naked beneath her robe.

All I would have to do was walk toward her and open that belt, let the fabric slide to the floor, and then

. . .

An ache of need rushed to my groin, and my jaw ticked. "This isn't going to work," I said, clenching my hands at my side. This was a shit thing to do. I knew it, but damned if I could stop myself.

"I . . . I don't know what you mean." She shook her head. "I just—"

"This. You working here. It just isn't going to work."

"Wait, I don't understand." She searched my face, her wide eyes glassy with a rush of tears. "Did I do something wrong?"

What could I possibly say? *No. I just can't control the insatiable desire to fuck your brains out.*

I stared at her, my blood still pumping as I tried to frame a coherent response.

"If you're still mad that I took Dylan out the other night without texting, I told you, I'd—"

"Not Dylan," I cut in, spearing my fingers through my hair in agitation. "You're great with her. It's just . . ."

With the groan of a man on the edge, I lunged at her, sweeping her into my arms and crushing my mouth to hers. It was the space of an instant, but it didn't matter.

Feeling her lips on mine, the sweet mint of her breath, the heat of her skin, it was all complete perfection.

She froze, and for a second, I wondered if she would pull away. It would be for the best, and I'd been such an asshole to her, I more than deserved her rejection. But just as I was about to release her, her lips parted and she molded her body to mine. If we went even one step further, I would be completely lost. We needed to talk first, and then?

Well, I'd see how things played out. I pulled away, the breath sawing in and out of my lungs even as my cock pulsed with need.

"It's not your fault, Addison. It's mine. I'm attracted to you in a way I've never felt before. Hell, I can't even think about seeing you in that bikini without wanting to fuck you senseless."

Her breath caught. I was still holding her, feeling the rise and fall of her breasts against my chest, and though her eyes widened, she made no move to step away.

"And then, after you told me the story about your ex and how he shook your confidence—" I shook my head, trying to loosen the words sticking to the insides of my brain. "All I can seem to think about is showing you exactly how much I want you."

She blinked up at me once, then twice, and I traced my thumb along the side of her cheek, willing her to keep looking at me, to give in, to confess what she wanted.

Electricity crackled between us and I held my breath, waiting for it to ignite a fire. Instead, Addison disentangled herself from me and tightened the knot of her robe.

"But you're my boss, Max. I know I haven't been here long, but I love your daughter and I don't want to lose this job if things get . . . sticky. So, where does that leave us?" She was practically breathless, her cheeks flushed, and she glanced down at the floor rather than look at me.

But I was done with that—done with playing cat and mouse.

I took another step toward her and tucked my fingers under her chin, turning her gaze to me. "I'm your boss Monday through Friday from nine to five. The rest of the time, we're a man and a woman."

She sniffed, pulling her chin away. "You're not serious."

"I am. At night, on the weekends? I'm not paying you for that time. Whatever happens then happens between two people, not a boss and an employee."

"And you think it's that easy to separate it all?" She raised her eyebrows.

"I don't see why it can't be," I shot back. "We both want this. And it only gets tricky if we let it. We like each other. We respect each other. We're friends who also want to sleep together. So long as we know that's what it is, surely we can manage to keep it casual."

"Casual," she repeated thoughtfully.

"I know what your ex did to you, and I know you're probably gun-shy after that, but I would never hurt you or make you feel like you weren't sexy or desirable. Maybe this—" I searched for the right word. "Maybe this arrangement between us would help you feel better about all that. I still meant what I said before."

"Max," Addison said on a sigh.

"Don't overthink it. We're two adults, and there's no

reason why we can't enjoy each other's company without it turning weird. Besides, living like this is hardly less weird, right? Tiptoeing around each other like a couple of teenagers with a crush?"

She pursed her lips, then ran the pink tip of her tongue over her full bottom lip. "Maybe."

"More than maybe," I argued, and I closed the space between us again, circling her waist with my arms. Lowering my face to hers, I kissed her again, slower and deeper this time.

Fuck, she tasted good.

She met my lips gently at first, shyly, but when I swept my tongue out, she opened her mouth for me, pushing and pulling along with me as our tongues danced together and our breath became quicker and shorter. My cock pulsed, growing impossibly hard, and I pressed myself against her, wanting her to feel exactly how much I wanted her, how I needed her.

"I have to think about it," she whispered as she broke away, gasping. "Dylan has to come first."

"I agree. Dylan comes first." I nodded.

"So . . . can I think about it? Just for a day. I'll tell you tomorrow, I promise." She disengaged from my arms again, her eyes hooded in what I could only hope was lust. "I just don't want to make a rash decision."

"I can respect that. So . . . tomorrow, then."

"Tomorrow." She nodded.

I backed away, my whole body tense with need, somewhat mollified that she looked as desperate as I felt. If this was what it took, waiting twenty-four hours for a chance to finally touch her the way I'd dreamed of? I'd dig deep and find the patience to wait.

I made for the door and descended the stairs, careful not to make eye contact with my friends. Somehow, I felt like if I looked them in the eye, they'd know what I was up to and try to talk me out of it, and that was the last thing I wanted.

If all went well, tomorrow I would finally get to see Addison naked in my bed.

A rush of need surged to my groin and I crossed my legs at the ankle, desperate to think of something else. Instead, my mind was humming with thoughts of

Addison.

How long had it been since she'd actually been with a man who wanted her? I considered this, but the idea of her being with another man at all had me balling up my fists and trying to change the subject inside my mind yet again.

I was so caught up that I flinched when Zach and Matt jumped up, cheering as our team rushed into the end zone. I leaped up to join them but my heart wasn't in it. When we sat again, Zach turned his attention to me.

"What's going on with you, man?" he asked.

I frowned in his general direction. "What do you mean?"

"I mean you're acting weird."

"I'm not," I argued.

"You are," Matt cut in. "What gives?"

"Just have a lot on my mind." I tried to focus on the TV again, but both my friends continued to stare at me, quietly sipping their beers and watching me like I was the main attraction.

"I think you've got nanny on the brain," Zach teased. "I can definitely understand that."

"Shut up," Matt barked at him. "She'll hear you."

"Exactly," I said.

"It doesn't mean he's wrong, though," Matt said. "You've clearly got the hots for her."

"She's attractive. So what?" I asked with a roll of my eyes.

"Other than the fact you live with her?" Matt asked.

"That's the least of your problems," Zach added. "Just look at her. She's all wholesome and subtly sexy— perfect girl-next-door type. Spells trouble, bro."

"What in the hell is that supposed to mean?" I shot back.

Zach shrugged. "Listen, just, good luck with that, buddy."

"No," I argued. "Spit it out."

Zach let out a little sigh. "Fine. All I'm saying is you have this gorgeous woman taking care of your house and your daughter. You don't just want to fuck her. You're growing dependent on her, and that means things can only get messy."

"Maybe for you it would," I said.

"For anyone," Matt cut in.

I ignored them both and focused on the game. Soon, they stopped yammering and followed suit, but their words stuck with me, playing in my mind on a loop.

Addison had said it, and Zach and Matt had agreed as much. Things between us could get very sticky.

But as my cock throbbed again at the very thought of her soft mouth beneath mine, I knew it was too late for doubts.

Because if I had a chance to get sticky with Addison?

I was sure as fuck going to take it.

Chapter Twelve

Addison

There's a reason he's still single at thirty-five.

Ever since Max had left my room a couple of hours before, the words had played through my head like a broken record. It didn't matter what I said or did to try to convince myself; it all just came back to that. He was ten years older than me. And my boss. It could only lead to trouble. Right?

Walking around the backyard, I picked up Dylan's toys and thought over everything that had happened earlier. It had been so quick—in the space of thirty minutes, I'd gone from being almost fired to being promoted to potential casual sexual partner.

Casual.

That must be his thing. After all, his tryst with Tiffany had been "casual" before he stopped it. And with Dylan's mom too. How many women had he been with that way? And how long did it take for him to get bored with them? He'd been with Dylan's mother for only a few months . . . was that a long stretch for him? Was that what he thought commitment was?

I glanced down at Mr. and Mrs. Potato Head lying together in the grass, their plastic hands touching in wedded bliss.

"How do you guys make it work?" I sighed. They looked at me with their lifeless eyes, and I scooped them up into my tote full of toys with a groan.

Okay, so what if he was a player? He said he wouldn't hurt me. And so long as I had my head on straight, he couldn't, could he?

Because what if he was right? What if all I needed to shake off this whole Greg thing wasn't to stay away from men, but to feel what it was like to be desired and wanted for the first time in years?

I pursed my lips and sank onto the bench of the picnic table where stuffed animals from this morning's tea party were still seated. All the glossy plastic eyes stared at me, and I picked up the teapot, if only to have something to do.

"I wish this was something stronger than imaginary tea," I muttered, and then poured myself a cup before offering it to the doll opposite me.

"He's a good man, a good father." He cared about Dylan so deeply that I could feel it when I watched them together. But then, if it didn't work out . . .

I stuffed my teacup into the tote, then ushered the rest of the tea party toys along with it.

How long had it been since I'd been properly laid? Every girl deserved fireworks, didn't she? Greg had certainly never delivered where that was concerned, and as for the other men in my past . . .

There hadn't been much of anyone to speak of. A few short relationships here and there, sure, but nobody real. Nobody who made me want to tear off my clothes and ride him like a rodeo bull.

Not like Max.

I'd never even had a one-night stand or one crazy, reckless night. And where had that gotten me?

Twenty-five and practically a virgin for all the times a guy had made me come.

I'd always thought it was me. That somehow I was just so bad at sex that I wasn't capable of getting to that point, but maybe if I gave Max a try . . .

God, just thinking about his hard cock pressed against me made me shiver.

I stepped away from the table and yelped when I discovered I'd stepped on a plastic tea set spoon. After stuffing it into the bag with everything else, I strolled in through the back door and set a pan of water on the stove to heat.

No matter what I decided, it was going to take some time to sort everything out. There was no doubt about that. I'd have to learn to live with the fact that his assistant—the woman he saw every day—had nearly been with him too, along with who knew how many women. That he wouldn't stay in my life forever. That it wouldn't be love.

But for me, it had never been love before. What difference would it make?

I pulled the items I needed for dinner from the fridge and set them out on the counter. A roar sounded from the living room, but I barely heard it.

Because I only had twenty-two more hours to decide

whether Max was worth the risk, and I had no frigging clue what to do.

Chapter Thirteen

Max

"And an extra-large order of fries. Do they supersize here?" I asked.

Zach glanced back at me, a stupid grin on his face. "Yeah, we got it the first couple of times you said it, chief," he said with a laugh. "Burgers, and as many fries as they'll give us. We're almost to the speaker now."

I stared out the window from the backseat, squinting at the too-bright drive-through sign. Why did it seem like there were two signs? I closed one eye until the second one faded.

"Maybe a burger too," I added. "And four chicken nuggets for Dylan."

"We told you, it's the middle of the night, man. Pretty sure Dylan is already asleep," Matt cut in.

"Shit," I whispered. "Did I call Addison? Did I tell her—"

"We've been over this." Zach sighed. "Matt and I called her before we left the office. She had no problem with you enjoying your birthday having drinks with friends."

"And boy, have you enjoyed it," Matt said with a snort.

I frowned. Even now, with the edges of the world so blurry, I could only remember bits and pieces of my night. The two of them had shown up at my office door an hour before I usually left, and insisted that I go with them to some shithole of a bar down the street. At the time, I'd agreed because it was just for one celebratory birthday drink.

But one drink turned into five. Then I lost count as we toasted everything from my thirty-fifth birthday to the quarterbacking prowess of Peyton Manning. The last thing I remembered with any clarity was clinking glasses and chugging a shot in honor of J.Lo's booty at the request of a howling Zach.

"You guys are a bad influence," I complained. I'd told the guys last week that I didn't want to do anything for my birthday, and not surprisingly, they hadn't listened.

"That's why you like us," Zach said as Matt, our designated driver, motioned for us to quiet down while he ordered. We pulled up in the pickup window's line, doubtlessly full of other people who'd been thrown out of the bars at two a.m., and I tapped my fingers against my jeans, a little amazed at the texture of the fabric.

How did I never notice that sober? They were so soft. Like unicorn fur.

"I still think you should have gone home with that girl," Zach said. "She said she was a nurse. You're going to need one tomorrow."

"I need one tonight," Matt murmured, holding up his hand for a high five from Zach.

"No, no, I don't want a nurse. I want Addison," I slurred, flopping back against the seat with a groan. "She's got great teeth. Have you ever noticed that?"

Zach blinked, then Matt reached out the window and then turned to hand me a bag filled with food.

"Eat up, buddy. It's for your own good," Matt said, and I stuck my hand into the bag, not bothering to look inside before I fished out a paper-wrapped burger.

I peeled away the wrapping, took a huge bite, and savored the meaty, cheesy goodness. I rarely ate fast food, and this was so hot and delicious, I found myself wondering why. I chewed, pausing only briefly to swallow.

"They're so straight."

"What?" Zach asked, shooting me a look over his shoulder.

"Addison's teeth. She's got a great smile. The other day she was smiling at Dylan, and I was just looking at her like, 'Whoa, that's a hell of a smile,' you know?"

Zach and Matt exchanged a look, but then Zach pointed to the bag and reminded me again to eat.

"You're going to need some water and aspirin when you get home too," Matt said.

"Addison will know what to do," I said with my mouth full. "She always does."

"Right." Zach sighed. "Okay, almost home."

We passed the rest of the ride with the guys talking about the nurse who'd hit on me. It was true, she'd been pretty—buxom and brunette with legs that looked like she might have been a dancer. She was exactly the kind of girl I would normally want to tie to my bed and keep there all weekend. But now, when I thought of my bed, I could only picture one woman there, naked on top of the sheets and waiting for me.

"Okay, we're here." Matt popped the car into park, and Zach climbed out to open my door for me.

"What am I, Cinderella?" I asked. "Get the fuck back in the car. I can walk myself to the door, Prince Charming."

Zach raised his eyebrows and barked out a laugh, pulling out his phone. "Right. You got it. But if you fall, note that I'm videoing you, and it'll be on Instagram inside three minutes for the world to see."

I flipped him and his cell-phone camera the bird and pulled myself from the car, momentarily surprised when the world spun around me as I stood.

"You sure you're okay?" Matt asked.

I frowned at him. "I'm fine."

"Be careful not to wake the baby," Zach reminded me in a singsong voice.

I waved them off. "Go home. I'm fine."

Before they could say anything else, I started for my

front door and listened as their car pulled away behind me. Without their headlights, it was pretty dark out, but the porch light was still shining. Addison had probably left it on for me. She was so thoughtful that way.

I fumbled with my keys, then opened the door and stumbled over the threshold. I didn't remember the door moving quite so quickly before, and it crashed against the wall beside it.

I winced. "Dammit."

A light clicked on in the living room. Addison peered at me through sleepy eyes, a book spread open on her lap.

"Were you waiting for me?" I asked, trying not to weave on my feet.

"What? No." She shook her head. "I fell asleep reading. You look like you had a fun night."

Her lips quirked, and I tried my hardest to remember why I wasn't supposed to cross the room and kiss her face, but nothing was coming to mind.

"Looks like you could use some water. Come on." She motioned for me to follow her, and I was careful to close the door quietly behind me before doing just that.

In the kitchen, she had a glass with ice water waiting for me, and was opening a bottle of ibuprofen I kept above the sink.

"I don't need that," I muttered, then gulped the crisp, cold water. I made a mental note to drink more water. It was so refreshing.

"Do it for my sake then," she said, holding out a few pills in her palm. I took them and popped them in my mouth, if only in hopes that it would make her smile at me with those straight white teeth of hers.

"Okay, time for bed, I think. What do you say?"

She strolled away and I followed her again, this time watching her curvy hips sway beneath her boxer shorts as she moved. My cock flexed, waking from its drunken slumber to weigh in on the view.

She led me up the stairs and into my bedroom. I flicked on the light as we stepped in. On the nightstand sat a single cupcake with a little "Happy Birthday" flag stuck into the perfect swirl of chocolate icing.

I blinked, staring at it in wonder. "Did you make that for me?"

"Dylan and I did." She shrugged. "It was nothing." Her cheeks turned a pretty shade of pink, and I stepped toward her.

"It's not nothing. You do so much for me." I took her hand, wanting to thank her, but the second I touched her skin, that damn electric pulse shot through my veins and I wanted to pull her closer, to smell the sweet lavender of her hair again. To feel her lips against mine.

There was a reason I shouldn't. I knew it was in there somewhere, but damn it all if I could think of it right now—especially not with her silky hair hanging down her back and her cute little short-shorts framing that perfect ass.

I glanced down at her hand, closing one eye again to stop the double vision, and wondered if it would be weird if I bent over and kissed it like they did in olden times. Luckily, she pulled it away from me before I drunkenly decided it wouldn't.

"Did you have a good birthday?" she asked.

"It was okay. I would have liked it better if you were there."

She raised her eyebrows. "Is that so?"

"Yeah. This girl came over to me and sat on my lap, you know," I murmured, suddenly enthralled with the graceful line of her neck.

Addison's mouth flattened into a thin line, but then she smiled. "Ah, so it sounds like a very good birthday then."

"No, I made her get off." I shook my head. "The only person I want on my lap is you."

Her eyes widened and her pink cheeks went crimson. "Oh boy, yep. Definitely time for bed."

"Listen, don't placate me because I'm drunk. It doesn't mean I'm not telling the truth." I took her hand again, this time pulling her close enough that her body was flush against mine.

She fidgeted, almost like she was debating whether she should move away, but I wrapped my arm around her waist and rested my hand on her lower back.

"I only want one birthday gift this year," I said. "And it's you."

I cupped her chin with my free hand and she stared

into my eyes, her expression torn, like she was at war with herself.

Time to see if I could help make up her mind.

I swooped down, crushing my lips to hers, and that sweet electricity sparked between us again, igniting something in me I wasn't sure I'd ever felt before. I pulled her body closer still, wanting her to feel the thick outline of my erection. She moaned a low, needy sound as her hips arched against mine.

I groaned in reply, rubbing against her so that my cock rode her slit in just the right spot. God, did I need to get inside her. Slide deep into that wet, hot warmth that I could feel branding me through the fabric of my jeans.

I lifted a hand to cover one of her breasts, my pulse cranking up as her nipple pebbled beneath my fingers.

To my surprise, her fingers trailed down my stomach, burrowing between us to cup my cock, running up and down over the fabric.

Fuck if I didn't want her to unzip me right then and there and slip her hand down the front of my boxers. I wanted her to tease me, stroke my swollen shaft up and down, and then get on her knees and do all the things I'd imagined her doing three times a day since she'd moved in here with me.

Instead, she gripped me one last time and then slid her hand away to grab my ass, pulling me close to her again. We were lost in each other, consumed by the heat of our mouths, the feel of our tongues as they slid against each other. I stepped back, drawing her with me until I felt the bed frame behind me, but misjudged and went tumbling backward. When the room finally stopped spinning and I opened my eyes, I realized I was alone on the mattress.

Addison stared down at me, her nipples hard, her chest heaving, and her eyes full of regret. "You're drunk," she whispered. "I'm sorry. It just doesn't feel right."

Fuck.

"But I want you," I said, knowing I was slurring my words even as I said it and cursing myself.

She shook her head slowly. "I know. And I want you. But not like this. We'll talk tomorrow like adults when both of us have had time to let sanity prevail." She pressed the back of her hand to her heated cheek, and then said, "Happy birthday, Max."

"Thanks."

I slumped back on the bed and watched as she left the room, my cock raging with unfulfilled need.

Happy fucking birthday, indeed.

Chapter Fourteen

Max

"Tiffany, would you bring in the largest bottle of Tylenol you can find?" I rested my forehead on my palm and tried to think of anything else I could do to ease the throbbing pain of the world's most epic hangover.

Luckily, I hadn't thrown up, or if I did, I definitely didn't remember. Which wasn't saying much because I already couldn't remember how in the hell I got home from the bar. I made a mental note to get in touch with Zach and find out.

Tiffany opened my door and rested a pill bottle on the corner of the desk. "Is that all you need?"

"Coffee," I croaked. "And . . . yeah, just coffee. From the deli across the street. It's stronger than what we have here."

Her brow furrowed with worry, but she turned on her heel and clicked the door closed behind her.

All morning, between hating myself for developing a taste for alcohol and cursing my friends for encouraging me, I'd been thinking of Addison.

Just before I left for work this morning, I came into the kitchen to find her eating a cupcake, the tiniest bit of frosting clinging to the corner of her mouth. I wanted to walk over and kiss it away, then taste the sugar on her tongue.

Instead, I'd grabbed some coffee and asked, "Do you have any idea why I woke up covered in chocolate frosting?"

She gave me a wary grin. "No, but I do know when I put you to bed, I left one on your nightstand."

"Drunk eating." I groaned. "Is there anything worse? Judging by the ketchup on my shirt, I'm guessing it wasn't the first round of it either."

"A time-honored tradition," she said with a nod and shot me a wink.

"Tell me I didn't do anything stupid," I demanded, dread already building in my gut.

"Not that I know of. I didn't talk to your friends when they dropped you off, but you did say . . ." The color in her cheeks rose and she said, "You asked me for a very particular kind of birthday gift."

"Ah," I said carefully. "I see." I'd told her I wanted her a few days before, so there was no point in walking it back now. "Well, I can't say that I regret that. Especially when I still don't know your answer. Did you tell me last night?" Had I been so drunk that I wouldn't remember something so fucking imperative? The thought was chilling. "Jesus, did you decide what you want to do and I missed it?"

She swallowed another bite of her cupcake and shook her head. "No, but—"

"You know what? Let's talk about it tonight."

I felt like a prisoner who had been given a stay of execution. After her seeing me behave like a stumbling fool, I needed at least one more chance to redeem myself before she made her decision. She nodded, and I scooped up my briefcase and headed for the door before she changed her mind. I was in such a rush to get out before she changed her mind that I brought the ceramic coffee cup to my truck with me.

It didn't matter, though.

I needed to focus on tonight. I had to do something so perfect and Addison-inspired that she couldn't possibly turn down my proposal. All I had to do was figure out what that thing would be.

Normally, if I needed something like this, I'd ask Tiffany to handle it—she picked out the best flowers and fruit baskets, and I obviously had no idea what I was doing. But when it came to Addison? Well, I knew that wasn't an option. If I wanted to win her over, I was going to have to do it myself. She deserved no less.

As the day went on, I put together the pieces. I called in an order to the grocery store and to the florist. I picked out a special bottle of wine. I was going to do this right, and by the time I got home, I was filled with single-minded determination.

While Addison changed Dylan, I rushed around the living room, picking up the toys and even vacuuming before she got the chance. When she came back down, I told her to relax in the living room while I handled the kitchen. She protested, but eventually she did as I asked.

I cleaned the stove, the counters, and the tiles, and by the time I got to cooking, I cleaned as I went along too.

"What are you up to in there?" Addison asked as she tried to walk toward the stove, but I waved her off.

"Nope, dinner is a surprise. You spend time with Dylan."

While I cooked, I could hear her in the other room, playing with my daughter, reading her books and showing her how to stack blocks, and my stomach clenched.

This time two weeks ago, I would have been cracking open a beer and ordering takeout for the thousandth time. Or maybe I would have been bringing home some random woman to warm my bed for the night, the only sort of company I'd kept until now ... now that Dylan was here.

And if I was being honest with myself, now that Addison was here.

Looking back, I felt sort of bad for my old self—the lonely, restless existence that came from flitting from one woman to another. Having nothing to come home for.

That was the way it had been with Jenn too. I'd thought back then that she was my girlfriend, but even that label had me skirting away just as fast as I could. And had she actually been a girlfriend? Not really. Thinking on it now, I realized I hardly knew anything about her. She would just come over, share a quick fuck, and then stare at her phone while we ate takeout. She never asked about my dreams, and I never asked about hers. We were together, but also apart. Strange that even then I knew it wasn't something I wanted for life.

That wasn't companionship or a relationship at all. It was just mutual loneliness.

Still, it was the most long-term relationship I'd ever had. Besides Jenn, it was only one-night stands and flings I could barely recall now. As much as I might have enjoyed a woman's company, none of them had ever had the kind of energy and warmth Addison brought into the house.

She was just so damn easy to talk to—like I could share my darkest secrets with her and she would understand everything I said. She shared about herself too. She'd told me about her stupid ex and her mother, and let me into her world.

Only a few nights ago, we'd been sitting together on the sofa, watching something on TV, and she'd tilted her head to the side. "It must have been really hard to find out you'd be a single parent the way you did."

I'd nodded. "I guess it was, yeah."

"Most people have nine months to prepare, but you didn't even have that. And looking at you and Dylan? You'd never know it."

"What makes you say that?" I asked.

She pointed at the TV. "I was just thinking about the nanny on this show. She's pretty much the only parent. That's the way it was for my nanny, but it's really not like that for me. You're a good father."

My heart stuttered. "Thanks. I didn't know you had a nanny."

She nodded, still staring at the TV. "She actually sort of looked like this lady."

The woman on the screen was chubby and kind-looking, with salt-and-pepper hair and an easy smile.

"My mom made her wear a stupid uniform too." She shook her head. "She was a single parent, like you. But she did her best."

"Not exactly a ringing endorsement."

"Science waits for no man. Without a father around, my mom couldn't really follow her dreams and spend all her energy on raising me. It wasn't her fault."

"Wasn't it?" I'd asked.

She'd glanced at me, a shadow of sadness tinged with regret playing over her face. "Every parent is different. I just want you to know that you're a good one."

A trill of laughter sounded from the next room, interrupting my memory, and I smiled to myself, picturing the two girls together. If I didn't know better, they might have been mother and daughter. So easy and comfortable together, almost instantly.

"All right, dinner is ready." I called them in, then swept my hand out toward the buffet I'd created.

"Whoa." Addison smiled as she walked into the room with Dylan on her hip. "What's all this?"

"Breakfast for dinner. You've made pancakes two times in the past week, so I thought—"

Her grin widened. "I guess my secret is out. They're the only way to eat cake for breakfast while maintaining your dignity, so they're pretty much my favorite food."

"I guess so." I cut up a pancake for the baby and sat her in her high chair while Addison loaded her pancakes with the fresh berries and homemade whipped cream I'd made.

"I had no idea you could cook," she said.

"I got a little help from Pinterest," I admitted, and she laughed.

"I told you it's addictive."

I joined her at the table with a plate, and we talked about our day.

"How's the hangover? Gone or still nursing it?" she asked around a mouthful of food.

I grinned and tucked into my own stack. "Yeah, it was a rough morning, but by lunch I was fine."

"You really didn't have to cook and clean like all this," Addison said, but I shook my head.

"I wanted to. You work hard, and I want you to know how appreciative I am."

Her eyes went suspiciously soft, and she looked away.

For the next little while, the three of us ate and chatted, Dylan piping up with some happy squeals as I mashed up a strawberry for her. Addison and I cleaned off the table and sat back down with cups of decaf coffee while the baby played on the floor with a set of pots and pans. It was the most domestic evening of my life, and I was happier than a pig in shit. Who knew?

Now if we could just end this night on the perfect note . . .

"Dylan's head is bobbing already, so if you want to put her to bed and then unwind while I do these dishes, that would be good."

"You can't be serious. You—"

I held up a hand. "Not negotiating."

She looked down at the sink full of dishes and then at Dylan. "I'll pay you back for this."

"You will not," I countered.

She picked up the baby and carried her from the room, allowing me to watch her hips as they swayed. Something buzzed in my pocket and I flinched in surprise. That would teach me for letting her body hypnotize me so completely.

I glanced down at the screen and saw a number I didn't recognize.

"Probably some telemarketer," I grumbled, but I answered just in case. "Hello?"

"Hey," a familiar female voice said on the other end of the line, and I nearly dropped my phone.

"Jesus, Jenn? Where the hell are you?" Fury, panic, and frustration all filtered through my mind, but I couldn't decide which one to pick.

"I'm around. I just wanted to see how you and Dylan are doing."

"And you didn't think to do that the day after you dropped her in my lap? Or maybe any of the days since?" I snapped.

Silence crackled over the line before she blew out an annoyed sigh. "Max, don't—"

"No, you don't. You don't get to dump her off like a sack of flour and then call a week later and ask anything about my daughter."

"*Our* daughter," she said quietly, correcting me.

How was she so calm? It was like she was completely without feeling, reciting a speech she'd written long before this call.

"You brought her here and left. That makes her my daughter now, Jenn."

There was a pause on the line, then she continued as if I'd never spoken. "Did you find the medicine I left in her diaper bag? She had some bad diaper rash and—"

"I've been taking care of her. The diaper rash is gone," I snapped.

She breathed a sigh of relief. Relief. Like all her problems were solved. "That's good to hear. Is she eating well? Asking for me?" she asked hopefully.

Asking for her? Like Jenn needed the validation of Dylan crying for her mother for her own selfish reasons. The thought sent a bolt of hot fury through me, and I gritted my teeth. "I'm hanging up."

"I wish you wouldn't. I don't want to intrude; I just want to know how you're all doing. Are you managing?"

I clicked the phone off and then stared at it, dumbfounded.

Where did she get off? I should have been the one asking questions. *Why did you leave? Why did you keep her a secret?*

And the one that made my heart squeeze with dread.

Are you going to come and take her back from me?

Instead, I had to carry on with my life wondering when the ax would drop, if it ever would. The thought made me sick. All I could do was hope that the fact that Jenn had stayed away this long meant she was happy with her choice and confident in the knowledge that I would do whatever it took to keep Dylan with me.

Upstairs, the pounding of the shower halted, and I focused back on the present. I couldn't let Jenn take tonight away from me—she'd already taken too much, like the entire first year of my daughter's life. Tonight had been a dream I didn't even know I had. Life was too short, and there were too few moments like this to let fear of the unknown steal it away.

For now, my sole focus was Addison.

And I was going to make damn sure she knew it.

Chapter Fifteen

Addison

I stepped into the shower and breathed in the hot steam, hoping it might give me some clarity. I couldn't lie—it was nice to have Max handle all the little details of dinner and the house so that I could relax, but . . .

How the hell was I supposed to relax?

I turned, allowing the rush of hot water to pound down my back as I closed my eyes. I'd had a full forty-eight hours to argue with myself about whether to go along with Max's proposal, and I was still just as confused as I'd been when he'd propositioned me. I'd even nearly called Lara a few times for moral support, but every time I was on the brink of thumbing the DIAL button, I put my phone down again and flopped back on my bed.

I knew what she'd say, of course. She'd parrot back exactly what I'd told her the last time we'd talked. That it was bad business to sleep with the boss, and a one-way ticket to homelessness. But she hadn't met Max. She had no way of knowing what a difficult choice it was, how impossible it was to look into his dark eyes and not give him everything he wanted.

Opening my eyes, I reached for my loofah and scrubbed until my skin was pink and tingling.

I hadn't called Lara because I didn't want to hear her, just like I didn't want to hear the part of my brain that told me not to imagine what it would feel like to be lying on a bed, naked and exposed to him, and to have his hot, muscular body braced over me. To feel his thick shaft rubbing against my entrance, to feel him move inside me with all the command and force I knew he would.

My nostrils flared and I tilted my head back, allowing the spray of water to coat my hair and rinse away the stubborn bits of Play-Doh still stuck in it.

The real problem here was Dylan. Dylan came first. Even Max had agreed to that.

But there was no way of knowing how things would turn out, and in turn, affect her. And if Max changed his mind about wanting things to be casual . . .

Then Dylan could have a mother again. I would be her mother.

Warmth rushed through me at the thought, but I beat it away. I was getting ahead of myself. All I had to do was get out of the shower, get dressed, and make a choice about tonight.

I knew what I wanted to do, and I knew what was smart. But at this point, it looked like Max and I would find out at the same time, because I still had no fucking clue which I would choose.

I turned the tap until the water stopped, then dried myself off and slipped into the soft cotton dress I'd brought into the bathroom with me.

It was unusual for me to dress in anything other than pajamas after a shower, but after all Max had done tonight, I wanted to look nice for him.

Not because I was going to say yes, but because this sort of felt like a date. Not that it was a date either, it was more like . . .

I sighed. I was confusing even myself now. God only knew how it would sound when I tried to explain how I was feeling to Max.

In my bedroom, I sat in front of my vanity and whipped my semi-wet hair into a bun on top of my head. Normally, that would do it, but then . . .

He'd cleaned and cooked for me. He'd been so sweet.

I glanced at the tiny pink makeup bag, then opened it and pulled out a few essentials. A dab of concealer, a coat of mascara, and lip balm, and I was ready.

Was this why he'd done everything around the house? Because he wanted me to feel beholden to him? Like that might convince me to sleep with him?

I shook the thought away.

That was something Greg might have done—if, in fact, he'd had any interest in sleeping with me. He used to manipulate me all the time to get what he wanted, but that didn't feel like the kind of move Max would pull. He was just trying to make me feel special, and I wanted to make him feel special in return.

That was all.

I took a deep breath and stood at the top of the steps, willing myself to move. Downstairs, I could already hear the gentle chords of a familiar song, though I couldn't name it off the top of my head. Steeling myself, I walked down to find Max sitting in the living room, a fresh bouquet of roses and daisies on the coffee table in front of him.

"Wow, those flowers are beautiful," I said.

"They're yours. Something to say thank you for everything you've done for Dylan and me."

I smiled. "If you're going to get me weekly gifts for doing my job, then—"

"It wasn't your job to redecorate her room like that. I just wanted to show you how much I appreciate it."

I drew my bottom lip between my teeth, sucking hard. "It was no problem at all."

"Then it won't be any problem accepting the flowers either."

I rolled my eyes. "Do you want more coffee or . . ."

"There's a bottle of wine uncorked and ready for you in the kitchen, if you want it."

"Right." I nodded. "Thanks. Do you want—"

"I've already got some. Hair of the dog, and all. I just didn't want to ply you with alcohol unless you wanted it."

Wanted it? I was pretty sure that was the only way I was getting through this night. I rushed into the kitchen and poured myself a healthy glass, focusing again on the music. The voice was crooning and sweet.

When my glass was ready, I walked back into the living room. "I thought you were strictly a Bob Dylan guy. You like Elvis Costello too?"

"I like all good music."

His gaze met mine, and I had half an urge to hightail it back up the steps. He was looking at me like he was a lion and I was a gazelle. Or, more particularly, like he was a starving man and I was a juicy slice of cherry pie.

I swallowed and then settled in beside him on the couch.

"You didn't send me any messages today. I was convinced you and Dylan had fled to Peru," he said.

"We talked about it, but Dylan wasn't interested. She had some spit bubbles to blow and a ladybug to try and eat. Maybe tomorrow." I laughed.

He chuckled and took a sip of his wine. "So, what else did you guys do?"

"Oh, you know, we read some Clifford and then we went to the pet store to see the real Cliffords."

"No kidding. What did Dylan think?"

I grinned, remembering her reaching her chubby fingers out to one of the brown-spotted puppies. "She kept pointing to the puppies and calling them babies."

Max grinned. "Tell me you're not hiding a dog somewhere in this house?"

I shook my head. "Not yet, but it was a close call. I think Dylan named every dog in the store."

"Oh yeah?"

"Yep. Most of them are named ball, but a couple are confusingly named bird."

He laughed again. "Sounds about right. I was 'ball' for the first two days we were together."

I tilted my head to the side. "Yeah, I could see that. Your head is very round."

He fake scowled at me and I grinned.

Silence fell between us then, and I combed through my memories of the day, trying to think of something cute

Dylan had said or done so that we wouldn't get down to the crux of the matter—not just yet, at least. Nothing was coming, though, and Max was starting to look at me with that intense, hungry gleam in his eyes again. I knew what he was thinking, what he wanted.

I took a gulp of wine for courage.

"So," he said.

"So," I repeated, my pulse beating a quick rhythm.

"Have you thought about my proposition?" he asked.

Have I thought of anything else?

I should say no. Maybe if I say no, he'll give me another day, or maybe a week. Enough time so that I'm not a complete chicken the next time he asks me.

"I have."

"And what do you think?"

"I think . . ." My mind tripped through the words, picking the first few that jumped out. "I think I don't know. I think I want to, but I . . . I also don't want to."

He nodded, thoughtful. "And what makes you not want to do it?"

"I'm nervous about Dylan. If something should happen between us . . ." I couldn't bring myself to finish the sentence.

"Do you think I would let the personal matters between you and me interfere with my daughter getting the best care possible?"

"Well, no," I admitted. "But feelings can get messy, and people behave all sorts of ways they don't intend to. What if it gets weird and you decide to let me go? I'm sure there's someone else just as good who can—"

"Nobody is as good with my daughter as you are. You two are inseparable. I know that, and I wouldn't let you go for anything that happened between us, ever. Let's get that straight."

"Oh," I said. The tips of my ears heated, and I knew it wouldn't be long until the heat spread to my cheeks again, a sure tell that he'd flattered me.

His lips tilted to the side. "So that's the reason you don't want to. What makes you want to do it?"

I blinked at him, incredulous that he'd even have to ask. "The way you look at me. Nobody has ever looked at me like that." I shook my head, trying to find a way to express myself that was true, but not too corny. "I'm curious, I guess. To be with a man who knows what he wants and who can make me feel . . ." *Like my whole body is on fire?* "Like a real woman," I finished, my voice husky with embarrassment. "Who makes me feel desirable."

Heat sparked in his eyes, and he nodded. "That's only because you are desirable."

Slowly, he took my wine from me, brushing his pointer finger gently against mine. Even at that slightest touch, my arms broke out in goose bumps, and I was practically panting as he reached across me, setting my drink on the table and allowing his masculine smell to take over my senses.

Then he turned to me, taking my hand in his and looking so deep into my eyes, I was sure he could see through me.

"Let me show you."

Now was the moment. It was my chance. *Sink or swim.*

Holding my breath, I nodded, and he leaned closer

until his lips were only a whisper away. Then they were on mine and I was sinking. Fast.

His mouth was warm and inviting, and he wrapped his hand around the back of my head, weaving his fingers through my damp hair. It was gentle at first, almost like he was giving me one last chance to back away, but the second I felt his skin against mine, I knew there was no chance that I'd let him go. Not now that heaven was just a breath away.

His tongue swept out, and I opened my mouth to accept his invitation. Just as gently, he brushed his tongue along the bottom of my lip, teasing and coaxing me until I met him with my own. He twined his tongue with mine, pushing the kiss deeper until I let out a little moan of longing.

Already, the kiss wasn't enough. My heart was racing, my blood was pounding in my ears, and I wanted more. I gripped the back of his neck, willing him to understand what I needed.

As if in answer to my unspoken plea, he trailed a hand under my dress, moving past my thin lacy panties and sliding beneath my bra. With one hand, he massaged my breast, teasing and enticing, moving closer and closer to the center with each touch. By the time he finally took my nipple between his thumb and forefinger, I wondered if I might come right then and there.

His touch was electric, his kiss intoxicating, and even five minutes in, I had already forgotten why I'd had the urge to fight this perfect, pure ecstasy.

"Thank you," I mumbled against his mouth as he pinched my nipple harder.

He smiled against my lips. "Thank you?" He raised his dark brows as he looked at me, and my cheeks burned. "You're fucking adorable, you know that?"

Then he kissed each of my cheeks, soothing the scorching heat there, before returning to my lips and dropping his hand lower until he was at the hem of my lacy panties.

I moved to open my legs for him, to let him feel just how wet and needy he made me, but he only hooked a thumb under the elastic waistband, waiting there, teasing me until I was panting even harder than I had been before.

"Max," I murmured, though I didn't know what might come out of my mouth next.

"Come to bed with me."

I searched his gaze, knowing that this was my last chance to back out. But even knowing that, I couldn't think of a single reason to say no to him.

"Yes," I breathed.

He took my hand in his and led me upstairs, past my room and into his. It was more spacious than mine, though the walls and dressers were bare. On the bed was a simple blue comforter, and I debated for a moment what I should do, where I should go.

With Greg, I used to slip beneath the covers and undress where he couldn't see me, but based on the way Max looked at me—like he was drinking me in—I knew that wouldn't be an option this time.

Not with him.

I swallowed hard, readying myself to pull my dress away, but then my breath caught and I was transfixed, watching as he peeled off his thin black T-shirt. I could see every detail of the thick black Army tattoos on each of his biceps, see the way his muscles bulged as he moved for his zipper, the way his waistline tapered into a perfect vee below his six-pack.

I felt like a complete idiot, but my mouth was watering and my knees were weak like something out of a movie. I let out a little whimper, and then he pulled down his pants and boxers in one tug to reveal the biggest dick I had ever seen.

A rush of need surged between my legs, and I considered pushing him back against the bed right then and there. It had been too long since I'd had a man, way too long, and I'd never had a man like this one. Looking at him, I wasn't sure how the hell he was even going to fit.

His gaze followed mine and when he noticed what exactly I was staring at, his mouth tilted into a slight smile.

"Don't you worry, baby. This is nothing you can't handle, and I'll make sure you're more than ready for me."

Chapter Sixteen

Max

I stared at her, wondering if she could see my heart beating out of my chest. But if she could, she showed no sign of it, too distracted by everything else I had to offer.

Never tearing her gaze from me, Addison licked her lips and nodded as if she'd made an agreement with herself. Then slowly, she sank to her knees in front of me and took me in her hand.

"Ah, fuck no," I groaned, though I hated myself for stopping her.

Her eyes went wide and wild. "What? Did I do something wrong?"

"Not at all. God, it's so fucking right. But I want to see you." I pulled her hand away from me and urged her up until we were face-to-face. "All of you."

Slowly, gently, I lifted her dress over her head and let it fall to the floor beside me. Her underwear was white, lacy, and simple, the perfect accent for the girl next door. It made my cock throb just looking at her.

I lowered my mouth to her throat, trailing kisses from the hollow of her collarbone to the shell of her ear as I twisted the clasp of her bra and allowed it to fall away. I wanted to pull back, to look at her, but I had to take my time.

Instead, I wrapped my hand around the back of her neck and whispered in her ear, "Now the choice is yours. If you want to go through with this, you can take off your panties." I slid my hand over the lacy fabric, feeling the wetness that dampened the front. "If not, you can still turn back."

She hesitated, her stiff nipples brushing against my chest, and then she lowered herself again, this time sliding her panties off as she moved and stepped out of them at last.

Now I could see her, all of her—from her pretty pink nipples to the glistening pink flesh between her legs.

"Now, get on the bed," I said.

"But I . . ." She glanced at my cock, swiping her tongue over her lips again.

I squeezed my eyes shut and said a prayer for

strength. If anyone ever heard about this, I'd have to turn in my man card, but fuck, I really did want it to be perfect. Everything either of us had fantasized about. I was already a man on the edge, and having her suck me off and blowing into her mouth early was not what I wanted.

"There'll be time enough for that. I want to look at you."

Taking both her shoulders in hand, I guided her until her knees buckled against the mattress. She scooted back, her knees still together, and I took a deep breath, ignoring the surging need in my cock for one second and allowing sanity to prevail.

This really was the point of no return. It was likely a terrible idea, I knew—between my baggage and my commitment issues, this was a recipe for disaster. It was all the more clear to me now, looking at her slender form as she lay in my bed.

But that was the point, wasn't it? She was already in my bed now, willing and waiting for me, and even though I hadn't had her yet, this still felt better than any woman I'd ever been with—it felt right. I couldn't let her walk away, not now.

Maybe not ever.

I shoved aside that terrifying thought as I glanced down at her closed legs, then met her gaze. She was staring at me still, waiting for me to come closer. She pulled her bottom lip between her teeth, and for the first time, I realized that the blush on her face trailed all the way down her neck to her breasts. She was as pretty as a fucking picture.

I held one of her knees and she slid her legs apart, showing me the pretty pink space between her thighs.

"Fuck me," I groaned. It was the most beautiful pussy I'd ever seen, and I couldn't wait to bury my face between her legs and make her beg for me. I was nearly on the point of doing just that when she interrupted me again.

"You should know it's been a while for me." The redness on her cheeks and breasts deepened. "So . . . be gentle, okay?"

I crawled between her legs and cupped my hand behind her head, pulling her lips to mine. She met me timidly, and I brushed a strand of her hair away from her face.

"Don't you worry about a thing," I said. "Tonight, I'm taking care of you."

I placed another tender kiss on her lips and she returned it, pressing her hand against the plane of my chest, then raked her nails down my pecs. I let out a little grunt of pleasure and she startled again, looking like I'd struck her.

"Did I—" she asked, but I shook my head.

"You won't do anything wrong. Not when you're with me," I murmured. "I want it all, whatever you got. Whatever you want to do, I want in. Don't hold back, Addison, because I sure as fuck don't intend to."

She held my gaze for a long moment and then nodded. This time she pulled my face to hers, kissing me tenderly and gently, like every move was a word of praise picked especially for me. We moved together slowly, ignoring our racing hearts and focusing on the feel of our mouths against each other, our tongues entwined in the push and pull that was just the start of what we wanted— what we needed.

As she kissed me, I held her in my arms, pressing my chest against her full breasts and savoring every moment when her breath caught or quickened.

I couldn't remember the last time kissing had felt so intimate, and it seemed like we'd been locked in each other's arms for an eternity before Addison drew away from me.

"I want you," she said, her voice raw and needy. "I want you now."

"Not yet." I shook my head. If she hadn't been with a man in a while, there was one thing I knew I had to do before we made love, and I was bursting at the seams to do it.

Slowly, I kissed my way down her body, stopping to massage her tits and suck on the cherry tips of her nipples. She gasped as I released each with a pop and then she whimpered, begging me for more, but there was no chance of that—not this time. Instead, I moved lower, kissing the neat triangle of brown hair above her pussy.

Then, when I was face-to-face with her pretty pink sex, I licked my way along her folds until I found the bundle of nerves at the top.

She yelped, gazing down at me with raised eyebrows,

and I grinned back up at her.

"Do you want me to stop?" I asked.

She shook her head and dropped back onto the bed, her hands gripping the comforter on either side of her hips.

"Relax." I kissed her again, lapping my tongue over her core before finding her nerve center again and coaxing it with my tongue. With my every little move, she quivered, her knees buckling. My cock ached so hard that I was shocked my eyes hadn't begun to cross, but I couldn't take her—not yet. Not until she'd come at least once.

With one finger, I pushed inside her and felt the sweet wet warmth I knew was waiting for me there. She was beyond tight, and as I moved my finger in and out, she bucked against me, pushing me deeper, riding me harder. All the while, I kept kissing her, rolling my tongue over her clit, loving every little shake and gasp and moan.

"Oh, Max," she rasped. "Max, I . . ."

But I didn't know what she was, because she let out a low moan that grew louder and louder the harder and faster I fucked her with my finger. Her walls jerked and quaked around me, and I pushed another finger inside as she yelped with pleasure.

"Oh my God, I'm, I'm . . ." She gasped.

"Say it, baby. Tell me what you're feeling," I muttered, my face still buried between her legs.

"I'm coming so hard," she said on a whimper. "Don't stop fucking me, don't stop. I need your cock. I want you to feel me come."

Fuck.

Dirty talk slayed me. Who knew Addison had it in her? God, did I want to put something else in her . . .

My cock ached with its own pulse as she rode out the aftershocks against my mouth. I glanced up at her, sorely tempted to climb up and bury myself deep. But I knew that if I fucked her now, there was no chance it would last for as long as I wanted it to. I wanted to know every little whimper and sigh she was capable of.

So I brought her back down slowly, playing with her, lapping at her and teasing her until I felt every last fizzle of her orgasm. When she finally quieted, I moved to her breasts, raking my nails over the tender underside of her curves, and sucked long and deep on her sensitive nipples.

"You have perfect tits," I murmured, and she ran her fingers through my hair.

"When are you going to stop teasing me?" she asked, tugging on my short locks.

"When it suits me." I shrugged.

She sat up, dragging my lips away from her, then pressed her core to my throbbing shaft. Moving her body up and down, she whispered, "Please, Max, I want you to fuck me."

My brain went offline for a second, the wet heat of her deep-frying my thoughts. My dick was like a wild beast now, raging, throbbing, and so heavy with need that it hurt. There would be other times for me to learn every inch of her. I needed to fuck this woman more than I needed my next breath.

Cupping her chin, I moved her lips to mine and kissed her slowly, gently, as I let her back down onto the bed. When her back was against the mattress, I gripped myself and teased her opening, rubbing my thick head around her clit until she writhed beneath me.

"Please," she gasped as she broke away from my kiss, and I held her face again, gazing deep into her eyes. This was the moment.

After what had felt like forever, Addison was going to be mine, all mine.

Settling back on my haunches, I pulled a condom from the nightstand and rolled it over my aching dick, then teased her again, taking a deep breath before finally, slowly, pushing just the tip inside.

I took her an inch at a time, watching as her eyes widened and her mouth opened into a perfect little *o*.

"*Fuuck*, you're so tight," I groaned, and she squeezed tighter against me, making me feel like I was going to lose my damn mind.

"You're so . . ." She panted, then grabbed my face with one hand, pulling me down to kiss her again. "You're so big," she whispered against my lips. "You feel so good."

I smiled against her mouth and pushed deeper still until I was buried to the hilt, and she let out a little whimper of satisfaction.

"Tell me if I hurt you," I said, and she shook her head.

"You feel amazing."

"So do you." I kissed her again, then drew back, still slow.

It was driving me crazy, moving inside her like I was trapped in quicksand, but I needed her to find herself first—to find the time to match my thrusts with the move of her hips, to kiss me in time with the growing need surging inside both of us.

But I shouldn't have worried about that.

With every little quake and move, she rolled her hips along with me, following my pace easily and seamlessly. Her tongue swept out to meet mine, and as she kissed me deeper, I knew she wanted more, wanted all of me.

Holding her in my arms, I moved faster, pistoning in and out of her as she tightened even more around me. I didn't think it was possible, but I felt even harder than I had before, and I buried my face in her neck. I sensed her climbing toward the edge again, her body tensing, readying for another climax.

Her nails scraped against my back and I sucked the silky skin of her neck, needing to claim her as my own.

Our breath caught and we moved in a frenzy, gripping any part of each other we could reach. I massaged her breasts, pulling back to fuck her deeper, and she grabbed for my bicep, my arm, anything in her reach.

"I've never . . ." She gasped, shaking her head. "I've never had it this good. That cock is perfect. You're amazing. You feel—"

I cut her off by bending down to nip hard at her straining nipple again, and she grasped me tighter, the one warning sign before her walls collapsed around me and I felt the long, full quake of her orgasm.

"Yeah, baby, come for me," I growled, fighting off my own explosion so I could ride hers out.

"I want you to come with me," she rasped breathlessly. "I want to see you."

Damn, if that wasn't the sexiest thing she'd said all night. Pulling back, I grasped her hips and pulled her into me, fucking her hard and deep until my balls drew up and the hard knot of tension in my stomach loosened, sending waves of euphoria throughout my body. Her pussy milked every last drop from me, tight and needy, sucking me dry. If I had any lingering doubts about whether this was a good idea, they were instantly wiped away.

She was better, sexier, tighter than any woman I'd ever been with, and as the last ripples of our orgasms climbed through us, I stared into her eyes, wanting to share the intense, sweet moment with her.

She stared back at me and I knew she felt what I did—that this was special. That it had been perfect.

In the silence, we panted together for a few minutes. Then I pulled away from her, removing the condom and dropping it into a nearby wastebasket before coming back to bed.

"What do we do now?" she asked, crossing her arms over her chest, looking more vulnerable than I'd ever seen her before.

I moved toward her, uncrossed her arms, and then tweaked her nipple.

"Get over here and lay with me," I said.

"I should probably sleep in my own room, but I can stay for a little bit." She raised her eyebrows, a grin tugging at her lips. "Never took you for much of a cuddler."

"I'm not. But I might be tonight if you let me be the big spoon." I climbed over her, then pulled her back to my chest and draped my arm over her naked body. Breathing deep, I took in the scent of her skin, of her hair, of the sex that still lingered in the air around us.

Fucking perfect.

"I'd say that went pretty well," she said.

"I'd have to agree." I kissed her hair. "And now I know for sure that I was right. Whoever made you feel less than in bed was out of their fucking mind."

She snuggled closer to me. "Thank you."

"No, thank you." I cupped her breast and she giggled, then turned to look at me.

"I really think this might work," she said.

"I have no doubt."

"But can you do one thing for me?" she asked.

"What's that?"

"Never make pancakes again." She grinned and wrinkled her nose. "I don't know how, but you managed to make them crunchy and mushy at the same time."

I laughed. "Family tradition. Not my fault if you can't appreciate it."

"Maybe that's one tradition Dylan can live without?"

"Maybe." I pushed a strand of hair from Addison's face, then stared into her eyes. "I'm sort of hoping she doesn't get much from me, anyway."

"What do you mean?"

"I don't want her to be part of the military family bullshit I got dragged into. It's nice, I think, and it's not because she's a girl or anything, but I want her to really make an impact in the world. The military is great, and if that's the path she chooses, that's fine, but—"

"It would scare you to death?" Addison asked.

I should have known she'd see right through me. "That obvious, huh?"

She grinned. "I think most parents feel that way.

They have a certain idea of what their kids should be or what they should do. My mom wanted me to be a surgeon. The day I told her I wanted to be a teacher, I think she almost had a heart attack."

"Oh yeah?"

She nodded. "Some people say teaching is the noblest profession, right? Well, my mother . . . doesn't feel that way. She thinks science is the be all and end all." She shrugged. "It's fine and it was her choice, but I think as long as you don't impose that will on your child, they'll end up just fine."

"Maybe so. But you and me—our parents did do that. So, what does that mean for us?" I asked.

"I guess we're screwed." She smiled.

"Guess so. I don't think I mind too much, though."

"Me neither. When I think about being a parent, though, I think more about what my mom did right than what she did wrong. She had a lot of pressure on her. I think if I was in her shoes, I would have done about the same," she said with a shrug.

"And what if you had things your own way?"

"I don't know yet. I'm not a parent. What about you? What's the dream?" she asked.

I considered her for a minute. I'd never thought about my future much—aside from how I wanted the company to do, at least. But now that Dylan was around . . .

"I want a big family someday, I think. A wife who loves Dylan like I do. Some more kids. Big Christmases."

She nodded. "It's a nice dream."

"Thanks."

Silence settled over us for a moment, and then the bed creaked and Addison sat up. "Speaking of dreams, I should be getting to bed."

"All right, yeah."

I couldn't ignore the faint disappointment I felt, but I stood, following her to the door and waiting as she collected her clothes. If we crossed into the realm of sleepovers and sharing a room, there was no going back. We had agreed to take things slow and keep it casual for now, and I wasn't about to back out on the deal already.

"This was fun," she said.

"You could do better than me."

She winked. "I could. But I like you and I love Dylan, and nobody is going to pry me away from her." Then, on her tiptoes, she kissed me, short and sweet. "Good night."

"Good night," I said, and when she was gone, I closed the door after her.

I should have felt like a million bucks. Tonight had gone great.

But there was something else, something that gnawed at my stomach. It might have been that I'd gone out on a limb—I'd never dated, after all. It could have been the risk I'd taken. More than that, though, it might have been what Addison had said. She loved Dylan, and Dylan loved her. It could be the start of something great for us all. And I . . .

Well, I was going to have to hope that I didn't fuck everything up like I always did.

Chapter Seventeen

Addison

MAX: How's your day been, pretty lady?

I stared down at the text glowing back at me and couldn't stop the grin spreading across my face.

> *ADDISON: We've had an amazing day. The baby just successfully put all the shapes in their proper holes, entirely unassisted. I don't want to call it too early, but I'm predicting a prodigy.*

I shifted Dylan from one hip to the other and set the phone down to pour myself a second cup of coffee.

It had been a long night. Despite having gotten to bed before midnight, I had tossed and turned until the wee hours, replaying every moment with Max in my head.

It had been perfect. Magical, even, as corny as that sounded.

My face literally hurt from smiling so much, and it

was getting to the point that I knew I had to cool it before we went for our afternoon walk. If strangers saw me looking this crazy happy, they might think I'd escaped a padded room and stolen someone's baby.

I took a long sip from my cup, expertly navigating it away from Dylan's busy little hands. "No, no, sweet pea. Hot, remember?"

She gave me a three-toothed jack-o'-lantern smile and nodded once. My heart melted, and I smooshed a kiss to her smooth, plump cheek.

I couldn't remember ever feeling this happy and satisfied with my life. Of course, the second I had that thought, a dull sense of worry burrowed in behind it, but I shoved it away.

Nope. I refused to be the worrywart who shat on everything good for fear of the other shoe dropping. Seriously, Max and I weren't even an item yet. We'd decided to take things slow and see where we ended up. Even if it didn't work out, we agreed.

Dylan came first.

I thought back to my interview with Max, and a sense

of unrest swept over me.

That one dark cloud had been hanging over me this whole time, and I wished like hell I'd handled it differently. When he'd asked about my training and education, that had been the time to come clean. Let him know that, yes, even though I had enough credits to graduate, I still had one more class requirement to get my teaching certificate, and life had gotten in the way.

Probably, it wouldn't have changed anything. I'd still have gotten the job and it would have been fine. Hindsight was as clear as day. But I'd been desperate and terrified to lose the opportunity, and now?

I shot a glance at Dylan and sighed. Now I just couldn't take the risk.

My phone buzzed, and I set my coffee mug down to grab it.

MAX: *Speaking of fitting the right piece into the proper hole, you busy later?*

It was followed by a hilarious-looking eyebrow-waggling emoji that had me belly laughing.

I tapped out a quick reply.

ADDISON: *Very smooth, Mr. Alexander. As romantic as that was, I'm still pretty sore from yesterday, so I might need some more convincing.*

I was still chuckling at our playful banter when the doorbell rang a couple of minutes later.

"I wonder if that's the new changing-table pad I ordered for your room," I said to Dylan as I sat her in her high chair and touched a finger to her nose. "Be right back, lovey."

The skip was back in my step as I peered out the peephole. The woman standing there didn't look like a UPS delivery person to me, and I frowned.

She was gorgeous. Dark blond hair fell in soft curls over her shoulders. Full, high breasts strained from a too-tight T-shirt, a pair of second-skin jeans clung to her curves, and her makeup was flawless.

I swung the door open and pasted on a polite smile. "Hi, there. How can I help you?"

The woman blinked her wide eyes once, then twice, before the answer hit me like a brick to the side of the head.

Dylan's mother.

Until now, I'd always thought that Dylan looked like her daddy. She had his expressions and that same little dimple in her chin. But as I stared at the woman I now knew to be Jenn, I realized I'd been dead wrong. Dylan was the spitting image of her stunningly beautiful mother.

The air left me like a popped balloon, and I tried to think of something . . . anything to say.

Luckily, she saved me the effort.

"Who are you?" she asked, eyeing me warily up and down.

It took all I had not to run a hand through my mussed hair. That was, until I realized I was wearing a baggy AC/DC T-shirt and a pair of faded leggings I'd had since college.

"I'm the nanny. My name is Addison." I opened the

door wider and waved a hand to usher her in.

From what Max had told me, the woman wasn't a psycho, and he hadn't told me to keep her out. It hardly seemed my place as the new nanny to tell the woman who had given birth to Dylan that she wasn't welcome, but at the same time, Max hadn't said to allow her in either.

I cursed myself for not pressing the issue harder when I'd thought of it early on. He'd seemed so sure she was out of the picture . . .

"Hi, Addison, I'm Jenn. Dylan's mom." She stepped into the foyer and glanced around.

I followed her gaze and wanted to weep with relief as I saw the place through her eyes.

It was clean, but also looked lived in. The blanket fort near the couch and the makeshift pots-and-pan drum kit made it very clear that the baby and I had spent some fun time together, a fact that made me feel marginally better.

"I saw the resemblance right away," I said, leading her into the kitchen, wondering if I was doing the right thing. "She looks just like you." I shot a glance at the clock and realized Max would be home within the next half hour, and he could make that decision for himself.

Jenn squealed as she caught sight of the baby, who was playing with a cone and a set of colorful rubber donuts in graduated sizes.

"There's my girl!"

I stood to the side, my stomach pitching wildly as I waited to see what would happen next, telling myself not to feel hurt no matter what. This was Dylan's mother. Yeah, Jenn had left her here, but that didn't change the fact that she'd carried Dylan for nine months and then raised her for the first year of her life.

But Dylan barely even looked up before going back to playing with her toys.

Jenn's mouth went tight with what looked like irritation, but I was sure must be hurt, and I instantly felt awful for her.

"She's probably just tired," I announced with a dismissive wave. "She's decided that two naps a day are for wimps, so we've been working through her cranky time in the afternoon. Dylan, your mommy is here. You want to come out and say hi?"

She perked up as I held my arms out to her and tugged her from her high chair.

Jenn held out her arms expectantly, but Dylan shook her head.

"No."

This was getting more awkward by the second. I shot a glance at my phone, wondering if I should sneak away and call Max after all. I didn't want to leave the baby alone with Jenn, but at the same time, I was starting to wonder if I'd made a mistake by even letting her in.

Jenn's pretty face was flushed with what looked like irritation, and I held the baby more firmly to my hip. This was not the tearful reunion I'd have expected at all.

"Does Max know you were coming, or should I give him a call and let him know you stopped by?"

"I spoke to him last night, actually."

That sent me reeling as a thousand thoughts attacked me at once. Why hadn't he told me about her call? He'd had more than one opportunity, both last night and this morning when we chatted over breakfast and he'd given me a quick kiss good-bye. Even a text could have worked if he'd forgotten.

But he hadn't forgotten. That would be a pretty big thing to not recall.

Which meant he'd intentionally hidden it from me.

There were only two reasons he would do that. One, if that call from her was something more than just a call and he didn't want to hurt me, or if my feelings on the subject didn't matter at all because I was just a quick fuck to him. And both options made me want to throw up.

The last remnants of joy drained away, and I cleared my too-tight throat.

"Yes, well, he mentioned he would be home early tonight, and should be pulling in within the next hour. I was about to start dinner. Maybe you'd like to play with Dylan and chat with me while I do that?"

She nodded and took the baby from my arms almost defiantly. For a second, Dylan struggled, and I wondered if I was going to have to fight this woman, but then she settled in.

"Aw, see? She just needed a second to remember

who her mama was."

I turned away so Jenn couldn't see that her aim had been true and her pointed barb had pierced my heart.

She wasn't lying. Facts were facts, but, God, did it hurt.

I tried to make small talk as I bustled around the kitchen, prepping chicken-and-veggie stir fry. It was a difficult task, though, as what I really wanted to say was never far from the tip of my tongue.

Who the fuck could leave this precious child?

How dare you come waltzing back in like nothing happened?

Can you please go back to wherever you came from and never return?

That was selfish and I knew it. If Dylan could have both her mother and her father in her life, that would be ideal. I had to put her needs before my own, no matter how much it hurt.

When the front door opened a few minutes later, I was a ball of seething emotion and an inch from tears.

"Hey, whose car is—" Max broke off as he stepped

into the kitchen and his mouth dropped open in surprise. "Hi, Jenn. Uh, what's going on?"

"I missed my little girl," she said simply, patting Dylan's bottom awkwardly as she squeezed her closer.

I watched the interaction more confused than ever. The way she was looking at Max, like he was what was for dinner, made me wonder if her visit here had been about Dylan at all. One thing seemed clear that made me feel marginally less horrible. He obviously hadn't known she was coming tonight.

Max shot his gaze from me to Jenn and then to Dylan, who cooed with delight and kicked her feet. His puzzled face morphed into a smile as he set his briefcase down and took his daughter into his arms.

"Hi there, little bear. Daddy missed you." He kissed her cheek and shot a warning look at Jenn. "We'll talk after dinner."

I should have taken that as my cue to go. Instead, glutton for punishment and not sure how to handle any of this, I stayed. The next forty-five minutes was a pain I wouldn't wish on my worst enemy as I watched Jenn fawn over Max, taking every opportunity to bring up their past together.

She was refilling his wineglass as she let out a peal of laughter so shrill, it sent a chill up my spine. "Remember that time we went to Cabo and you drank so much tequila, you climbed onstage to play the maracas with that mariachi band?"

He smiled and nodded, forking in some chicken and then pausing to give Dylan a bite of rice.

"I don't, actually, but I have the pictures to prove it."

"We had some good times . . ." Jenn trailed off and covered Max's hand with hers.

"Okay!" I blurted, and then pushed myself away from the table, pasting on a fake grin. "So, I'm going to go make some phone calls and let you guys . . . do whatever it is you guys plan to do with your night. Jenn," I turned and offered her a little wave, "it was nice meeting you. Max, give me a yell if you want me to do bath time with the baby."

I ran out of the room like the hounds of hell were chasing me, but even at that, I still didn't make it to my door before the tears started.

Shit, shit, shit.

How had I let myself fall so hard so fast? For Max, and for Dylan. And now it might all be over before it had even started. He didn't seem receptive to Jenn's come-ons, but be wasn't exactly putting her off either. And none of it explained why he hadn't mentioned the call, or more importantly, why he hadn't pulled her aside and demanded to know what she was doing here the second he walked in.

I swiped a hand over my face and chewed on my bottom lip.

This was crazy. I needed to get a grip.

I had just managed to talk myself out of tears and into anger when there was a knock at my door.

"Come in."

Max stepped into the room, and I sucked in a steadying breath as I took a seat on the edge of my mattress.

"Is everything okay?" he asked gently, his eyes filled with concern.

"Um, not so great, actually." I tried not to stare at his

muscular tattooed arms because all that did was make me wish they were around me, comforting me right now. "I'm just a little thrown off, and felt like I was interrupting family time down there." I managed to bite back an acidic comment about strolling down memory lane, but it was a close call.

Not my place to say. None of it was.

"I'm thrown off too. Addison, I had no idea she would show up."

"She called you yesterday. She didn't mention it then?" I asked.

He had the grace to look ashamed as he shrugged. "I should've told you that, but it was a nothing conversation. Certainly not one that indicated she would be coming back into the picture anytime soon."

I was a child who'd never had the luxury of having parents who lived under one roof. So, as much as it killed me, I had to do what was right for the baby. If that meant stepping back, that was what I would do.

"Maybe it's for the best." My throat ached, but I pushed through. "If Dylan can have you both in her life, she should. I don't want to get in the way of that. Go back downstairs and enjoy the time with your family, Max. I have some things to do, anyway."

He hesitated, raking a hand through his hair with a groan of frustration. "This is new territory for me, and I have no idea how to handle it. None of this came with instructions, Addison. Please, give me a chance to think it all through before you write me off, okay?"

"Last night was probably a mistake anyway, Max. It was a hot fantasy, and now real life is back, you know?"

He drew back and his face went tense, but he didn't reply.

"Go ahead, go back down and be with your daughter and her mother. We can talk another time."

I turned away and closed my eyes, not opening them again until the door closed a minute later. Then I dropped my face to the bed and screamed hoarsely into the pillow.

So what if Max had given me a couple of orgasms? None of that mattered now. It wasn't like I was his girlfriend or we'd made promises. I was just the nanny.

And it was time I started remembering that.

Chapter Eighteen

Max

I stared at the file in front of me and realized I'd read the same line a dozen times and was still no closer to comprehending it than I was when I'd started.

Fuck.

This whole thing with Addison had me in knots, not to mention the drama that had ensued afterward with Jenn.

Restless, I tapped my fingers on my desk and wondered where to go from here.

I knew where I wanted to go. My thoughts instantly drifted back to the other night with Addison. She'd been amazing. Responsive, sexy, and every curve of her body made my cock throb just thinking about it. More than that? I liked her. Really liked her. She got my sense of humor, and we got along so well.

Which was why I was still feeling stunned that she'd basically given me the brush-off.

I picked up a pencil and started absently drawing

cubes on the manila file folder.

Addison been almost chilly when she'd basically told me last night that it had been a mistake. It sure as shit hadn't felt like a mistake to me, though. Then this morning, I'd thought about talking to her. Telling her what had transpired between Jenn and me after she'd gone to bed, but she had refused to even look at me aside from wishing me a quick and not very convincing good morning.

A knock on the door scattered my thoughts. I looked up to see Tiffany standing in the doorway, a smile pinned to her lips.

"Hey there, boss man. How are things?"

I shrugged and smiled back. "Fine, how about you?"

Her grin dimmed and she stepped into the office, closing the door behind her.

"Who do you think you're fooling, Max? You never doodle like that unless something is bugging you. Did I do something wrong?" Her brows knitted together in puzzlement, but I shook my head.

"No, not at all, it's just. . . ." I wasn't sure of the

protocol here, but I could definitely use a woman's perspective, and the brief little thing between Tiffany and me hardly classified as a relationship. Surely, since she was my friend and assistant, it would be okay for me to get her take on this whole mess. "Jenn came over last night."

Tiffany's eyebrows shot high as she sank into the chair across from me with a gasp. "*Jenn* Jenn? Your ex?"

I nodded grimly. "Yeah. It was super awkward. She didn't tell me she was coming, and I think her showing up like that out of the blue upset Addison."

Tiffany's eyes narrowed and she stared at me speculatively. "Why would that upset Addison?"

The question caught me off guard. Why, indeed? If Addison didn't care about me, and the other night had been a mistake, then it should have been a relief if she thought Jenn was coming back around. Unless she was really just that upset about the potential of losing her job. Not that I could blame her. Dylan had only been in my life a short time, but already, the thought of losing her felt like losing a limb.

"It's complicated," I said finally. "And I've got a meeting to go to that takes precedence over my personal life. Sorry, I shouldn't have said anything. What's up? What did you need from me?" I asked, eyeing her expectantly.

Tiffany seemed to hesitate, like she wanted to say more about the subject, but then finally nodded. "I just wanted to remind you about the meeting, and let you know that I ordered lunch from Benito's for you guys to have in the conference room."

"Thanks," I said, genuinely grateful that at least one thing in my life hadn't turned to shit overnight. Tiffany was a good employee and was always looking out for me.

She waved off my thanks and stood. "If you ever need to talk or blow off some steam, Max, I'm here for you. We can grab a drink . . . and talk. Just remember that."

She backed out of the office and closed the door behind her, leaving me staring after her.

That was strange. The phrase *blow off some steam* had been one she'd used once to refer to what had happened between us a couple of years back. I was sure it was unintentional, but the way things were going, I couldn't help but wonder if I had one more complication on the horizon.

I set down my pencil and picked up the folder, intent on getting through the rest of the day focused on work. If I didn't get my head together, I wouldn't have to worry about Addison at all because I wouldn't be able to afford a nanny or that house.

The next few hours flew by as I dived headlong into work. When I finally came up for air just before quitting time, one thing had become abundantly clear to me.

Not even a full day had passed since Addison and I had talked, and I missed her already. I couldn't let this stand without at least trying to get to the bottom of how she was really feeling.

* * *

On the ride home, I thought of all the things I could say to Addison, but when I walked in the door a few minutes later, those thoughts flitted away like leaves on the wind.

The place was trashed, toys and sippy cups everywhere. Smears of what looked like chocolate—*please, God, let it be chocolate*—were on the living room wall, and a puddle of milk was spilled on the tile in the foyer.

"Hello?" I called, the very beginnings of fear starting to pulse through my veins.

What if Addison had fallen and gotten hurt? What if the baby had been by herself all day and I didn't even know it? Here I was all caught up in my own drama, and I hadn't even checked in on them. But my fears were laid to rest a few seconds later as Addison rounded the corner with Dylan in her arms.

"Hi," Addison said dully. Dark smudges were under her eyes, and her hair was caked with tiny ring-shaped noodles. "Someone is having a hard day today," she whispered.

Almost on cue, Dylan let out a bloodcurdling scream that rent the air.

"Teething, I think." Addison shouted to be heard as she tried to rock the screaming, stiff-with-rage baby in her arms. "Nothing has been helping."

I set down my briefcase and reached for Dylan. She quieted and came to me easily, snuggling close. The second I started to relax, she sank her three teeth into my neck. "Son of a—" I bit back a string of curses and tugged her away, holding her aloft in shock.

She stared back at me in full demon-baby mode, completely unapologetic as she stuffed her fist into her drooly mouth.

"Yeah, sorry. I guess I should've led with that," Addison said, pointing ruefully to twin teeth marks marring her collarbone. "It's not pretty. I was about to put her into the bath with some lavender oil to calm her."

Dylan's bottom lip started to quiver, and my gut gave a squeeze of sympathy. Even demon babies needed love. I held her close again, but not quite as close as last time, and kept my guard up. "Why don't you go relax for a while, and I'll do the bath, okay?"

Addison looked like she was about to argue, but then her eyes went suspiciously glassy and she nodded. "Yeah. I think I'll feel better once I have some tea, and maybe do some yoga or something."

She turned and I watched her go, feeling helpless and heartsick all at once.

How had my perfect little life gone to shit so fast?

I carried the baby upstairs, hoping against hope this was just a bump in the road and not the catastrophic end to something that had started so promisingly. Dylan and I would be okay. I'd make sure of it, but what of dealing with all of this? My lie of omission, Jenn coming by, Dylan pulling the exorcist routine—what if it was all too much, and Addison decided to get out while the getting was good?

The water was still running when I reached the bathroom, and I turned it off. Dylan whimpered softly as I made short work of her clothes and tested the water temperature before I slipped her into the tub.

The second the water hit her, she went quiet and I let out a sigh of relief.

I hated to hear her cry. Before I went to bed tonight, I needed to try to look up some more teething remedies because this shit was for the birds.

I knelt on the floor and rolled my sleeves up before setting a couple of her bath toys into the water. For a blessed few minutes, all was quiet. And then, it was too quiet. The sounds of her splashing and her bare bottom squeaking against the tub went still. The little cooing sounds she made as she moved her rubber ducky through the water ceased. And when I dared to look at her face, it was screwed up in intense concentration that could only mean one thing.

"No, no, nonononono!" I stuffed my hands under her arms and tried to lift her out of the water, but it was too late. Bubbles rose from the depths, followed by two brown logs that were definitely not chocolate.

"Addison?" I hollered as Dylan let out a peal of laughter. "Addison!" I called out again, frantic as Dylan's oil-slicked body slipped from my grasp. I lunged for her again, watching in horror as she reached out a chubby little hand to grab one of the floating logs.

She was just about to make contact when Addison pushed through the door and let out a gasp. "Shit!"

Her voice distracted Dylan just long enough for me to grab her and pull her from the tub. She plastered her soaking-wet body against me and laughed some more.

"Huh," Addison said, a smile finally reaching her tired eyes as she looked on. "I wonder if she was just constipated."

I let out a groan as she grabbed a towel and took the baby from my arms, swaddling her in it.

"How about you take her into your bathroom and give her a quick hose-down, and I'll take care of the floating logs of doom?" she asked, her lips quirking slightly in a way that made the ice wedged inside my chest start to melt.

She wasn't dumping us. Well, not Dylan at least.

It was a start.

I thanked her and rushed Dylan into the master bathroom to complete the bath-time ritual. Thirty minutes later, she was already nodding off on her changing table as I dressed her in her jammies.

"She's going to be out like a light," Addison said from the doorway.

I turned to see her there, looking like she might do the same.

"She didn't nap at all, so she's going to be pooped."

It was exactly that, some off-the-cuff remark that Addison probably hadn't even meant to be funny, that had me chuckling and then belly laughing a few seconds later.

"Pooped," I repeated, trying to keep quiet so as not to wake the baby.

Addison started laughing as well, and she held a finger up to her lips. "I swear to heaven, if you wake her, she's all yours. I'm shot," she whispered threateningly.

I nodded and lifted the baby, transferring her to the crib in one smooth motion. Addison and I crept out of the room like we'd just stolen something. We didn't speak again until we reached the living room.

"Well, that was something," I muttered, raking a hand through my hair and sending a pitying glance down at my soaked shirt. It was only when Addison let out a strangled groan that I realized the wet white cotton was totally transparent, and my abs and chest were on full display. I locked gazes with her, and her cheeks flushed pink.

Jesus fucking Christ. As bad as it all was, she still wanted me.

Thank you, God.

"Look, about last night—"

"You're my boss," she said swiftly. "You don't own me an explanation."

"But I want to be more than that. For real, Addison. So I need you to know, I don't think it was a mistake, what we did. I think it could be the start of something amazing. Don't walk away from that, please."

She stared at me and lifted a hand to her chest. "Y-you don't want to end it? I thought what with Jenn coming and all, that you guys were getting back together."

I wanted to kick myself for not forcing the issue last night and making Addison listen to me, but damn, she'd said she didn't want to be with me, so what would the point have been? Now, though, I realized there was no way I was giving up without a fight.

"She came to try to get me back. When I told her I wasn't interested but that we could discuss visitation with Dylan, she declined."

I still couldn't believe that Jenn had been so frank with me. So unashamed about her intentions and lack of love for our daughter, but there it was. The ugly truth.

I shook my head slowly and shrugged. "She just

wasn't meant to be a mother, I guess. She agreed that, all things considered, if we couldn't be together, it would be best if I take full custody of Dylan. She agreed to give it to me without a fight if I released her from any financial obligation. So I did. Papers will be signed next week."

It was twisted. I didn't want to be happy, because Dylan deserved a mother who loved her, but the truth was this was for the best. If the only reason Jenn wanted Dylan in her life was to get to me? That wasn't a mother's love at all.

"I'm sorry it happened that way, Max. I wish you'd said something. I was so worried about my own feelings, I didn't stop to consider how hard her coming here must have been for you."

I stepped closer, relief flooding me when Addison didn't pull away. "You had no way of knowing how things had gone down. I should've told you she called in the first place. Can we have a do-over?" I asked, tugging her close and closing my hands over her hips. "You get in bed tonight, drink your chamomile tea, and get a good night's sleep while I set the house straight. And then tomorrow, we start fresh. We tell each other everything. How we're feeling, what we're worried about, if we're feeling threatened, or even if we need some space. Complete honesty and a real-life, grown-up relationship. What do you say?"

She leaned up and kissed me on the mouth, but not before I saw a shadow pass over her face. "Yes," she murmured, curling her arms around my neck and hugging me close. "I want that so much, Max."

I squeezed her hard and then released her, stepping back with a groan. "If you're going to go, go now. My mind knows you're tired and overwrought, but my dick definitely doesn't give a shit."

She cocked her head, the shadow fading as an interested gleam entered her eyes. "I'm tired, but I'm not *that* tired."

"Nope," I said, using her shoulders to turn her around and usher her toward her room. "No way. I'm probably still harboring some sort of doo-doo parasites, and you have Spaghetti-Os in your hair, not to mention the fact that your eyes are crossing with exhaustion. Tomorrow, we're going to wake up to a new day. Clean clothes, clean house, clean baby—"

"Clean hair," she added with a laugh as she dutifully

headed down the hallway.

"And then, you and I can get dirty at night together," I added.

Addison turned and eyed me for a long moment, looking so intrigued by the thought that I almost dragged her back and bent her over something.

"Promise?" she asked.

"Oh, fuck yeah. Scout's honor."

And I couldn't wait.

Chapter Nineteen

Max

I stared down at the cookbook and groaned.

"Son of a bitch," I muttered.

Not only had I forgotten to add the butter, but I'd put in five tablespoons of flour instead of teaspoons. I picked up the bowl and upended it over the trashcan. Thirty minutes of mixing and measuring and whisking, all down the drain.

"Sum a bitch," Dylan muttered as she struggled to get hold of a rogue Cheerio on her tray.

I let out a groan and bent low until we were eye to eye. "Please, do Daddy a favor and don't tell Addison where you picked that up from, okay, pumpkin?"

Her eyes lit up and she laughed. "Assin?"

My heart beat double-time and I tickled her chin. "Did you say Addison? Say it again. Addison."

"Assin," she chortled back gleefully.

Okay, so maybe my raspberry soufflé was in the

shitter, but the baby had just said Addison's name for the first time. If my own emotional reaction to hearing it was any indication, Addison was going to be stoked.

I opened the oven door and peered in at the browning pot roast. It looked exactly like the picture in the book, and smelled like a home run. I just had to hope that I was enough for dessert.

The doorbell rang and I swiped a hand over the dishtowel I'd tucked into the waist of my jeans.

"Be right back," I murmured to the baby, heading for the door. I swung it open to find my mom standing there, her face full of anticipation.

"Where's my baby girl?" she said, pushing past me and swiveling her head around as she searched for Dylan.

"Hello to you, my wonderful mother," I said with a smirk, bending low to give her a quick kiss on the cheek. "Boy, it didn't take long for me to go from prodigal son to persona non grata, did it?"

She slapped my chest gently and rolled her eyes. "Don't be silly. You'll always hold a place in my heart, dear. She just holds the rest," she said with a wink. "Now, where's that little angel?"

I gestured to the kitchen and Mom scurried away. I joked about it, but the truth was, I couldn't be more thrilled about how quickly my parents had opened their hearts to Dylan. As parents, they'd been loving but reserved, attentive but strict. As grandparents? That tiny baby girl had them wrapped around her finger.

They'd only seen her a few times since she'd moved in with me because my father had gotten a stomach flu they hadn't wanted to transmit, but they Facetimed with us three times a week, and couldn't wait to get their hands on her again now that he was better. When I'd called to ask if they wanted to have an overnight visit, they were ecstatic.

It was going to be weird to be without Dylan. I'd become so accustomed to her being here, to hearing her sighs in the middle of the night and kissing her downy head in the morning. But tonight, after the rough couple days we'd had, I wanted to focus completely on Addison and whatever this was growing between us. She deserved my undivided attention because it was finally starting to hit me that this could actually be the real thing between us.

By the time I got back into the kitchen, my mother had already gotten Dylan out of her high chair and was shouldering her diaper bag.

"Don't forget. She doesn't like cold water, so give it to her room temp," I said, bending to ruffle my daughter's soft curls. "And she hates peas. If you try to give them to her, she'll spit them out and refuse to eat anything else. Also, no grapes unless you slice them l—"

"Lengthwise," my mother cut in dryly, shaking her head in mock disgust. "I swear, it's like you think you hatched from an egg fully grown. I got you through your toddler years just fine, so spare the lessons, kid." She hoisted the baby higher on her hip and bustled over toward me. "Now, give your mother a kiss good-bye so I can get out of your hair and you can try to seduce this nanny of yours."

I froze and stared at her in stunned disbelief. "How . . . what do you mean?"

"You said you needed a sitter for a date. I've seen and talked to your nanny during a couple of our Facetime visits, and you'd be stupid not to give it a whirl," she said with a shrug. "Judging by your face, I'd say I've confirmed my suspicions. Don't mess it up; she seems like a good egg."

With that, Mom wheeled around and made for the door again, disappearing as quickly as she'd come.

Don't mess it up, indeed. No pressure there.

The oven timer went off, saving me from having to think about that dire warning for too long, and I bent to take the roast out, releasing the scent of roasting meat and onions into the air.

"Oh my God, that smells like heaven," Addison said, stepping into the kitchen and tossing her keys onto the island.

I grinned and set the pan on the stove before turning to face her. "Thanks. I didn't even hear you come in."

I'd sent her off to get a spa treatment that afternoon, hoping it would scrub away the memory of pasta-hair and shit-water from the night before. Her glowing skin spoke volumes, but her eyes were glassy with tears. She swiped them away and forced a smile.

"I came in just as your mom was leaving. Boy, she is a real bundle of energy. She looks like a kid at Christmas."

"Yeah, she's excited," I agreed, my stomach sinking as I stepped closer and took her hand. "But don't try to distract me. What's going on? You're crying, Addison."

She let out a snort that turned into a broken sob, and my heart cracked in two. Not at all what I had planned for tonight. I just wanted to make her smile.

"Talk to me. Are you hurt?" I asked, pulling her into the circle of my arms.

"N-no. Oh God, it's so dumb. When your mom said hello to me, Dylan said my name. She called me Assin." She laughed again and then hiccupped. "You must think I'm a frigging idiot right now."

"On the contrary, I think you're so fucking amazing, you take my breath away." I pulled back and stared into her eyes. "And the fact that you love my daughter so much means everything to me."

"She's the best kid in the world," Addison said. "You didn't have to ask your parents to take her tonight, you know."

"I do know. But I wanted to." I lowered my mouth to hers, swearing to myself it would just be the one kiss for now. I'd planned to romance Addison, to feed and pamper her all night. But the second our mouths touched, it set off an avalanche of need, and I gripped her closer.

She opened her mouth and touched her tongue to mine, groaning as I pulled her closer.

So sweet . . . her skin was so soft. It smelled like honey and cinnamon, and I drew back and managed to grin down at her.

"You smell delicious. If that was a trap to try to get me to go down on you, it was a wasted effort. It's pretty much all I think about anyway."

Her cheeks went pink with pleasure and her gaze shot to my mouth. "You have a great mouth, Max," she admitted softly.

Her words sent a hot rush of blood to my cock and I dived back at her with a growl, this time going for her neck. I trailed my tongue over the silky skin and closed my teeth gently over her flesh as I let my hand roam up her rib cage to cover her breast.

Her nipple instantly hardened, and I rubbed it between my fingers. Her back bowed, pressing her closer against me, smashing her pussy tight against my needy cock.

Fuck yeah.

How could I have missed this so much when we'd only done it once before?

Damn, though, that once had been a mind blower. As I recalled how her cunt felt squeezing my fingers, dinner suddenly seemed like a waste of precious time.

"How hungry are you?" I asked softly, my lips still against her throat.

I felt the vibrations of her chuckle as she shook her head. "Not very. Why, you got a better idea?"

I shoved aside the mail that still sat on the counter from earlier that afternoon and sent it scattering to the floor like confetti. Then I gripped her waist and hoisted her up onto the countertop.

With her deep, throaty moan spurring me on, I yanked her shirt up, and with nimble fingers unclasped the front catch of her bra. Her pert breasts spilled forward and the breath whooshed out of me.

"You're killing me, Addison. It's like you were

plucked from my fantasies and put on earth to torture me."

I pressed my hand to the small of her back, urging her to arch forward as I caught the tip of one breast between my teeth. She curled her legs around my hips and let her head fall back as a moan escaped her lips. Realizing that I still had a free hand, I slipped it between us and shimmied her cotton skirt up a little higher. She cried out as I cupped her through the lace of her tiny panties.

I sucked hard, drawing her nipple deep into my mouth, laving it with my tongue before letting go.

"I can feel how fucking wet you are."

She let her head loll forward to meet my gaze. "You make me so hot, Max. All I can think about is how good it feels to have you inside me."

I curled my fingers around her underwear and yanked hard. She gasped, shivering as they came away in my hand. I let them fall to the floor and then cupped her waiting pussy. The wet heat branded my skin as I palmed her gently.

"Max," she breathed, shuddering as she wrapped one

arm around my shoulders. "We have all night. Just this once, hard and fast?" she pleaded.

I had sworn that this night would be all about Addison, and if she wanted hard and fast, hard and fast was what she'd get.

I released her and used both hands to yank at my button fly, tearing my jeans open and freeing my cock. It bobbed between us and I grabbed hold, pausing to gaze down at her bare cunt for a brief, perfect moment. I'd seen her before, but only in dim light. Here and now, she was so totally open to me, so wet and slick, it was like my daydreams had come to life.

I moved my hand up and down over my shaft, wishing I could be everywhere at once. Eating her pussy . . . pounding my cock into her . . . sliding my hands in her hair as she sucked me . . . watching her beautiful face flush with desire as I exploded, jetting hot cum all over those perfect tits.

Addison's eyes were locked on my hand as I worked my swollen member in smooth strokes until a bead of pre-cum glistened from the head.

"If you don't fuck me right now . . ." Addison

reached out to run her thumb over my aching tip, catching the creamy bead. I watched, light-headed, as she lifted her thumb to her mouth and sucked.

"Condom," I muttered, half in a trance as I stared down at her. "I have to go get—"

"I'm on the pill and was tested last month," she murmured breathlessly. "Are you . . ."

"Oh yeah," I growled in response. Dylan had been conceived despite condom use. In fact, this would mark the very first time I'd ever fucked without one. If felt so fitting to have it be that way, with nothing between us.

I pressed myself into her and arched forward, flexing my jaw to keep from letting a string of curses fly. Her cunt fit me like a glove, cupping me, squeezing me, milking me with every inch I fed her.

"God, Max." She gasped, rolling her hips and clutching at my shoulders. "You feel so good."

I tried to think, tried to keep it all controlled and together, but it was a lost cause. I groaned and gave in to the wildness, plunging forward as deep as I could go. She reached around and closed her hands over my ass, urging me on with wordless whimpers as I pumped into her, using her hips to guide her response, forcing her onto my cock again and again in long, deep strokes.

She began to moan my name, over and over, slowly, softly at first and then faster, and I rammed deeper.

"Take that cock, babe." I groaned, knowing how close she was, watching transfixed as her mouth dropped open and her eyes opened wide. "Take it all and let me feel you come for me. Let me feel it."

I slipped my hand between us to massage her slick clit with two fingers, and then it was over. She was screaming as she jerked and shook against me, her cunt closing over me again and again.

The sensation set off a firestorm, sending blood pumped through my veins as my cock jerked and fired off, spurting into her as I groaned her name.

"Fuck, Addison. So fucking hot."

We stayed like that for a long time afterward as our bodies recovered from the intensity. She moved first, swallowing hard and slumping forward to rest her face against the crook of my neck.

"Well, that was a nice welcome home," she said softly, chuckling.

Home. This *was* her home. The thought should have scared me, but it didn't. In fact, it made me feel warm somewhere deep down inside.

I wasn't about to ruin our first night completely alone with questions or pressure on either of us. Right now, things were perfect. This didn't require a label or some major declaration. Tonight, I just wanted to be with her and wake up with her next to me in the morning, then see how things unfolded.

"What do you say we eat some of this roast and then spend the rest of the night in bed, watching movies and . . ." I trailed off and let my gaze drift to her still bare breasts. Her nipples perked up instantly, making my cock twitch in response, and I wished I hadn't mentioned the roast at all.

"I'm definitely in for all of that. Especially the 'and' part," she said with a saucy wink.

I pulled back and helped her down from the counter, feeling better than I could ever remember feeling in my entire life.

If this was love?

I'd take it.

Chapter Twenty

Addison

"Monkey," I said, pointing to the baby baboon staring at us through the glass enclosure. "Can you say monkey?"

Dylan smiled and pressed her face to the glass with a squeal of delight.

"She was making monkey noises this morning when we were getting dressed," Max said with a chuckle. "I think she's just playing hard to get."

"Yeah, well, wait until I bribe her with ice cream." I swept her into my arms and pressed a kiss to her forehead before settling her back into her stroller. "I'm starving. Are you?"

I shot a glance at Max and tried not to melt. It was a warm day for late September, and he wore a faded Army T-shirt that bared his spectacular forearms and biceps, along with a pair of faded jeans. The other moms strolling by didn't even try to hide their swooning, and I couldn't blame them.

Other moms. You're not a mom, dummy.

Shit, I had to stop doing that. Over the past three weeks, though, it was getting harder and harder to separate fantasy from reality. That night after the counter sex and pot roast had been the first sleepover of many. In fact, now that I thought about it, we'd spent all but one night since then wrapped in each other's arms, and that one night had only been because I'd caught a milder version of Max's dad's stomach flu and hadn't wanted to infect the rest of the house with it.

We'd fallen into a rhythm, almost naturally alternating who got up with Dylan in the middle of the night, and then Max got up a few minutes before me to start our coffee. I'd even started making him lunches from our dinner leftovers, and it all felt so right.

"I could definitely eat," Max said, casually slinging an arm around my hips as we wound our way through the zoo.

This was my life now, and some days I wanted to pinch myself to make sure I wasn't dreaming.

Now if only I don't have to wake up.

"What do you want, chocolate or vanilla?" Max asked, stepping into line at one of the vendor trucks.

"Dylan and I will split a twist cone," I said, already missing the familiar weight of his arm around me.

It was like a fever, the need I had for him. No matter how many times we made love, it felt brand new. It had gotten to the point that I could have happily stayed in that house with just him and the baby forever and die happy. Which was exactly why I'd made plans with Lara for that evening, which was technically my night off. I didn't want space. If anything, I wanted to get even closer to him. To be able to say the words that were filling my heart to bursting.

I love you.

Which meant I definitely needed a little time away from them to get my head right, or I was at risk of rushing things and ruining what could be the best thing that had ever happened to me.

"M'lady," Max said, handing me the paper-wrapped sugar cone.

We made our way over to a little bench and sat together thigh to thigh as we ate and chatted. Dylan wound up wearing almost as much of the ice cream as she ate, but Max and I didn't care. It was lucky that our child-rearing style was so similar. Messes could be cleaned, and children should be allowed to be children.

I stroked Dylan's hair gently and my heart swelled. She was the center of our worlds. I never realized how much I could love a child until she'd come into my life, and for the first time, I knew I wanted a big family. Baby sisters for her to play with and baby brothers to tease her.

I pushed aside the thoughts before they dug in too deep. We were living for the moment. And right now, things were great. No point borrowing trouble or pushing things.

"Do you plan to stay in the city, or are you coming back home tonight?" Max asked, popping the last of his cone into his mouth.

"I was going to come home, unless you'd rather I didn't?" I shot him a quick glance, my stomach flopping.

"Oh, I definitely want you to come home. I just didn't want to assume." Max bent and gave me a hard kiss, a familiar light burning in his eyes. "I'll wait up."

***

As Lara and I caught up at our favorite sushi restaurant later that evening, those words replayed in my head, a sensual reminder of what I was going home to.

"Anyway, I told him that I didn't care if his divorce was almost final. He could call me when those papers were signed, you know?" Lara said with a snort. "I'm not interested in any of that type of drama in my life." She picked up her chopsticks and hoisted a massive piece of dragon roll into her mouth. Her cheeks puffed out like a chipmunk as she continued. "So, enough about my pathetic love life. Tell me, what's going on with Mr. Sexy Boss?"

I swiped my Alaskan roll through a little pool of soy sauce and then popped it into my mouth, buying some time as I tried to formulate how to explain things. Luckily, wasabi filled my nostrils and made my eyes water, which bought me an extra twenty seconds as I gulped some lukewarm tea.

"Um, yeah. So, we're together. Pretty much," I said, setting down my chopsticks and trading them for my cup of sake.

"Pretty much? What does that mean?" Lara frowned.

"Either you're together or you're not together, right?"

"Well, we've been sleeping together. In the same bed. And we spend most of our weekends and free time together."

She nodded, smiling. "Are you exclusive?"

The question caught me off guard, and I settled back into the booth with a sigh. Were we? I thought we were, but we'd never actually had the conversation. For all I knew, he could think we were still in the casual stage but just really enjoying each other's company.

"I don't really know," I said, hoping my cheeks weren't as red as they felt. "We're just, you know, taking it slow."

Lara's eagle eyes narrowed on my face and she gasped. "Holy fuck. You're in love already. Like, for real." She set her chopsticks down with a clatter and took my wrist, squeezing it urgently. "Don't try to bullshit me, Addison, we've known each other too long. You're crazy over him, aren't you?"

I didn't bother to deny it. Lara was right. From the day we met and she found me crying in the corner at the ice skating rink, we'd been besties. She'd sat down next to me, and we both froze our buns off while she pep-talked me like a pro. I waited now for that same signature pep talk, but something inside me quivered as I saw the worry lining her brow.

"What? Why are you looking at me like that?" I asked, tugging my wrist away.

"Oh, honey. When I see your face light up every time you talk about him or that baby, it makes me so excited for you. But it's been a month, and you guys are living together and playing house. You're head over heels in love, yet you have no clue where you stand. Weren't you the one who told me this whole thing started with a conversation about this being casual and fun? No commitment?"

I wet my lips and nodded. "Well, yeah. That's how it started. But—"

"But nothing. He was up front with you from the start, and unless he's told you otherwise, my fear is that you're setting yourself up for a major crash and burn." She released my wrist and settled back into her seat, gnawing on her bottom lip. "I know you can't unspill the milk here. You're in love, and that's not going to change anytime soon. But at least sit down and have a discussion with him. Be honest. Tell him you know this was supposed to be casual, but that you're falling for him, and if he's sure he won't commit, then you need to save yourself."

Save myself? Like . . . leave?

The thought made the sushi I'd eaten crawl back up my throat, threatening to make a reappearance.

"I can't do that. Leave Dylan?" *Leave Max?*

As terror shot through me, I realized I was even further gone than I'd thought. A life without either of them was almost unfathomable to me at this point.

Shit.

I hadn't wanted to scare Max away by telling him how I was feeling, but Lara was right. We'd promised not to do anything that would threaten my position in the house, and that Dylan came first.

Now, though, it seemed almost impossible to separate it all. If things ended, could I really go back to just being Dylan's nanny? And what, watch Max get ready for dates with someone other than me? No way. Those feelings would only grow stronger the longer we kept this up. If I had any chance of saving even a tiny piece of my heart from getting obliterated if he wasn't in the same place as I was emotionally, I needed to do it now.

I picked up my cup and knocked back the last of my sake, holding up two fingers for the waitress and wiggling them.

Later, when I got home, I was going to climb in bed with Max and live it up one more time, because tomorrow I had no choice but to ask him where we stood.

Which meant that tonight might be our last.

Chapter Twenty-One

Max

So good, Max, just like that. Ah!

Addison's low, breathy gasps replayed in my ears like the world's sweetest music, and I shifted beneath my desk as my cock thickened.

As much as we fucked, you'd think I'd get used to it, or at least be able to get through the day without thinking about it.

Not a chance. It was like the more we did it, the better it got. I knew her body now. Every delectable inch of it. What made her moan, what made her scream. Last night had been especially hot. When her Uber pulled up, I'd wondered if she'd be too tired, but when she'd stepped into the room minutes later wearing only her black heels and nothing else, I'd almost swallowed my tongue. She'd been buzzed, sure, but that didn't explain the urgency. The wildness of it. At one point, when I was pounding my cock into her from behind, I'd come so hard, I almost blacked out.

I reached a hand beneath my desk and gave the old

boy a squeeze, wincing. Five o'clock couldn't come fast enough. I'd ordered a massive bouquet of flowers to celebrate Addison's one-month anniversary as Dylan's nanny, and couldn't wait to give them to her. I'd even been super sneaky and stalked her Pinterest to get a bead on what her favorite blossoms were. Maybe I'd see if my mom could take Dylan for dinner, and Addison and I could—

"Hey, boss, got a minute?" Tiffany stood in the doorway, her expression dour.

Shit. If this was a work thing that was going to keep me here late . . .

"Sure, come on in."

She stepped in and crossed the room to sit across from me.

"What can I do for you?" I asked, sensing from Tiffany's body language that something was definitely wrong. I mentally kissed my perverted after-work sex fantasies good-bye and sighed.

"Actually, it's something I was doing for you," she said, handing me a sheaf of paper she'd been clutching in her hands.

I took it and stared down at it, frowning. "A college transcript? I don't get it."

"That's Addison's," she said softly. "You remember when you first were hiring her, you told me you put in an ad looking for someone with a college degree?"

Blinking, I stared at Tiffany, wondering what the hell we were talking about.

"Remember, you were excited about her education because she was a teacher?"

I nodded, my stomach tightening as I scanned the document.

"Well, when I met her that day at your house, something didn't feel right. I started poking around some and had a friend check into her for me. Max, she doesn't have her degree. She lied. Not only that, her last job was at a freaking café. How does that qualify her to take care of Dylan? And if she's lying about that, what else is she not being truthful about?" Tiffany leaned in and took my hand gently. "I just can't stand the thought of your leaving that sweet little baby girl of yours with someone who shouldn't be trusted."

My ears buzzed as the words sank in. Addison had lied to me?

"Max," a low, trembling voice called from the open doorway. Addison stood there with Dylan in her arms, her cheeks pale. "It's not what you think."

Tiffany let out a sharp laugh. "It's not? So you're saying you did graduate?"

"N-no." Addison propped Dylan on her hip and tucked a lock of hair behind her ear. "I didn't. But it was just a technicality. I had taken the wrong class and it didn't fulfill the requirement I needed, so I was three credits short. I had a 4.0. I just didn't have the time to go back and take the last class once I started working with my ex at his café. And then since I was short of credits, I couldn't get my teaching certification."

I stared at her in shock, my pulse hammering as I stood.

"Why didn't you just tell me? Lying on a résumé is one thing, Addison. But we shared a lot about our lives with each other." *And our deepest secrets, or so I'd thought.*

"And you chose to keep this from me this whole time."

"I thought you'd—"

"What? Fire you?" Tiffany said, glaring at her. "He should." She stood and walked toward Addison, reaching for the baby.

Addison jerked back reflexively. "Max . . ."

I was still reeling as I blinked at her, not sure what to say. "What did you come here for? Is everything okay with the baby?" I asked, my tone sharper than I'd intended.

"She's fine," Addison said, her cheeks still chalky white. "I just wanted to talk to you about something . . . it's nothing."

I tipped my head in a clipped nod. "All right, well, I think it's best if you go back to the house. We'll talk when I get home from work. Dylan can stay here for the rest of the afternoon."

Addison looked like I'd slapped her, but dammit, I was the one who'd been lied to. I needed a minute to get my thoughts together before I said something I'd regret.

Slowly, she handed the baby over to a smug-looking

Tiffany. Through the fog of my confusion, I made a mental note to revisit that with her. My assistant seemed way too pleased over this new revelation, and I wasn't liking it one fucking bit.

I watched, my gut churning as Addison wheeled around and scurried down the hall.

Tiffany cooed to an irritated-looking Dylan, and I made my way toward them and took her gently from Tiffany's arms.

"I've got her." I kissed Dylan's forehead and hugged her close. "You know, while I appreciate you looking out for me, I think the way you handled that with Addison was inappropriate. You overstepped, Tiffany."

She had the grace to look chagrined as she nodded, her cheeks flushed. "Sorry, boss. I was only trying to help."

She said the right words, but as I looked harder, I couldn't help but wonder if she wasn't sorry at all. In fact, her eyes still gleamed with triumph.

Once I figured out how to untangle this mess with Addison, I was going to have to decide how to handle

Tiffany. Between what she had done today and how she'd neglected to mention her visit with Addison earlier in the month, I was starting to feel like her feelings for me were getting in the way of her being able to work for me any longer.

Tiffany left my office and I closed the door behind her, groaning.

Everything had been peachy not twenty minutes before, and now everything was fucked. I wasn't sure who I could trust anymore. I had this perfect tiny little person counting on me to surround us both with people who could be counted on, and I couldn't help but wonder if I was failing her miserably.

I blew out a sigh and rested my forehead to Dylan's.

What the fuck was I supposed to do now?

Chapter Twenty-two

Addison

I stood in front of the bathroom mirror staring at my reflection, wondering how things had turned to shit so fast.

"It's your own fault," I muttered accusingly to the devastated person looking back at me through tear-blurred eyes.

As much as the whole coordinated attack in Max's office hurt, he was right. I had lied to him the day we met, and by not coming clean over the past month, I'd in effect lied to him every day since. But, damn him, he'd broken my heart today.

I could still picture the cold anger on his face as he told me to leave. Could still see the faint grin stretching Tiffany's lips.

"What a bitch."

There was no question I'd brought this on myself, but she'd made it a million times worse. And what made it even worse than that? The fact that I'd actually gone to Max's office today to tell him the truth and admit that I was madly in love with him.

Fresh tears slipped down my face as I turned away from the mirror and continued stuffing my toiletries into my suitcase.

I thought it had hurt when Greg and I had broken up, but compared to how I was feeling right now, facing the rest of my life without Max? That was like a paper cut. Now my heart felt like it had been stomped on by a herd of buffalo, and there wasn't shit I could do about it.

"Hey."

Max's voice jarred me from my thoughts, and I let out a gasp.

"I didn't hear you come in. Sorry, I'll be out of your way in a few minutes."

He glanced at the suitcase that was already stuffed with clothes, and his mouth settled into a grim line. "So you're leaving?"

I froze, staring at him like he'd lost his mind. "Of course. You and Devil Wears Prada basically fired me back there. What else would I be doing?"

I wanted to throw myself at his feet and beg him to

forgive me. To tell him that I never meant to deceive him. I'd been in a desperate place and knew I was capable of taking care of Dylan, but what was the point? He'd already proven back at the office that he didn't want to hear my excuses.

"I can't imagine this house without you anymore," he said simply. "And Dylan would be lost without you."

I refused to let those words give me even a glimmer of hope. The fact that his daughter loved me didn't change anything. "I wanted to talk to you about that. I know this is weird, but I'd like to be able to still spend time with Dylan once I leave. Maybe not right away, but in a few weeks, once a little time has passed." *And I can stop crying for more than three consecutive minutes.* "I'd like to be able to come take her to the park or something. I realize you probably don't trust me anymore, but at least think about it. She's lost enough, Max."

His eyes looked wild as he stepped closer and took my hands, using them to lead me out of the bathroom and into my bedroom.

"I can't concentrate on anything watching you pack that suitcase," he admitted with a low growl. "It's making me want to puke. And I also don't want you to come and take Dylan to the park once in a while."

I should have expected that, but it still felt like another blow to the solar plexus. "Please, Max . . ."

"No, Addison. It's me who should be pleading with you. I don't want you to leave at all. Stay. I was so wrong to handle things the way I did back there. All I can say in my defense is that I was shocked. Tiffany had literally just given me the news, and you walked in a few seconds later. If I'd had even ten minutes to let it settle in, I'd like to believe I would've handled it all very differently."

"So you're saying you want me to stay and continue being Dylan's nanny?" Joy and sadness melded together in a nauseating brew, and I swallowed hard. Could I do that? Could I stay here in this house and not be with Max?

"No," he said, running the tip of his thumb over the pulse in my wrist. "I want you to stay, but not as Dylan's nanny."

I was still trying to catch his meaning when he dropped to one knee and gazed up at me, his beautiful eyes blazing. "I want you to stay as my fiancée."

The world spun, my heart stuttering as I looked down at him in disbelief. "Are you for real right now?"

He gave me a sad smile and nodded. "I am. You gave Dylan your love, you gave us your time, you shared yourself with me, and after your past, I know that took courage. If you can't forgive me for the way I treated you back there, I understand, but I realized something today. I fucking love you. If I didn't, knowing that you lied to me wouldn't have felt the way it did."

Shame hit me almost as hard as his declaration of love. Was this really happening? "Max, I—"

"Let me finish. I should've thought about how much you've proven yourself to us, and how much I do truly trust you. So, here's my take on what happened. You were fully able to care for Dylan and knew graduating was just a formality. Then, the further things went, the more afraid you were to tell me." He frowned, his dark brows knitting together. "I don't like that you felt like you couldn't be honest with me, but then I realized that's partially on me. I should've made you feel secure. Told you how much Dylan and I both care for you and need you. Then you would've felt safe telling me, and you'd have known that something like that could never tear us apart."

He lifted his hands to rest on my hips and squeezed. "So put me out of my misery and tell me that you love me too. Tell me that we can put this in the past and move forward as a couple. Marry me, Addison. Please. We can raise Dylan together; you can go back to school if you want to. Whatever makes you happy. Just don't go."

My mouth was bone dry as I tried to get the words out. I went to speak, but a wail broke out in the next room.

Dylan.

"Shit," Max muttered with a wry laugh as he stood. "I put her in the crib with some toys so we could talk, but she's clearly done with them now. I know today has been crazy, so I want you to think about it. Just promise me you won't go."

I nodded. "Okay. Yeah, I'll unpack." I watched him leave, adrenaline from the roller coaster of the past few hours coursing through my veins.

As thrilled as I was that he'd said the L-word, I couldn't help but wonder if it had been a knee-jerk reaction to almost losing me. What happened if I went all in with him again emotionally and said yes, only to have him change his mind tomorrow? I'd done that. Gave Greg everything and more, and when he decided to pull the rug out from under me, I was left with nothing. I needed to be sure. Needed to be sure *Max* was sure.

He had offered me some time, so I would take it. I knew what I wanted. Max and Dylan, forever and ever. It was Max I wasn't so sure of, and the risk I was subjecting myself to scared the hell out of me.

I said a little prayer under my breath and set my suitcase back on the bed.

Please, God, let this be real. I don't think my heart could take it if it's not.

Chapter Twenty-Three

Max

Don't pressure her.

I stood in front of Dylan's door three hours after my proposal, crippled with indecision. Through dinner, bath time, and even a glass of wine, Addison hadn't said a word about it.

After the debacle at my office earlier in the day, I'd spent the rest of that afternoon kicking myself for being so hard on her. Especially in light of the way she'd embraced Dylan. She was as in love with my daughter as I was, and it showed in everything she did. Who cared about a few college credits?

Once I'd gotten over the initial surprise and realized I might lose Addison, it had become so clear to me that I wanted her in my life permanently.

But my "will you marry me" had been met with stunned silence. Not what I'd been hoping for at all. I could only hope that once she had a little time to think, she'd see how awesome it would be. The three of us together, like a real family. Who knew? Maybe it could even be the four of us someday . . . or the five of us.

That thought lessened the tightness in my chest a little.

I stood by Dylan's bedroom door and pressed an ear to it, slumping with relief at the sound of silence. She'd been fussy for most of the day at my office and had missed her nap, so I'd put her down early. The first fifteen minutes had been hell as she'd wailed and whimpered, even calling us by name.

"Dadaaaaa . . . Assinnnn!"

I'd sat outside the door in the hallway the whole time, wrestling with myself over whether to go in and get her, but Addison had been firm, saying that we should give her a chance to learn to comfort herself. Of course, she said that right before her eyes started to water and she ran away to hide in the kitchen.

I grinned in spite of myself. She really did love Dylan and would be thrilled to know that the wailing had stopped.

I rose on stiff legs and made my way quietly downstairs.

"She's out," I murmured to Addison, who sat at the kitchen table with a mug of tea before her.

Her shoulders slumped and she groaned. "Thank God. I can't stand to hear her cry like that. It kills me."

I stepped up behind her and laid my hands on her shoulders, digging my thumbs into her tense muscles. She hummed and let her head fall forward.

"That feels really good."

My pulse kicked up as I continued the massage. We'd both been in the house sort of drifting past each other all evening, lost in our own thoughts. Me worrying about whether she would say yes, and her, who knew? Maybe wondering whether she wanted to get saddled with a guy who'd never had a real relationship before and came with a lot of baggage?

Fuck, I didn't want to pressure her, but I wasn't even sure if I should be looking for a ring at this point. Maybe she was going to pipe up and tell me she didn't want to be with me at all.

I hated the uncertainty.

She reached back and squeezed my wrists gently,

stopping me. Then she stood and turned to face me.

"Since the baby is asleep, maybe you and I should hit the sack a little early too," she said, not meeting my gaze.

"Together?" I asked, hoping like hell she meant what I thought she did.

She nodded and wet her lips. "If you want to."

Oh, I wanted to. But I didn't bother with words. I just bent and swept her into my arms. She let out a low squeal and then slapped one hand over her mouth as we froze.

Silence greeted us, and I chuckled. "You almost woke the kraken," I whispered, carrying her past Dylan's closed door to my bedroom. I crossed the room to the bed and laid her gently down on the mattress. A devious thought tickled the edge of my brain, and I shot her a lethal grin. "Which gives me a great idea for a little game."

"Is it called 'Release the Kraken'? Because I think we've played that a few times already," she deadpanned.

The last of the awkward tension between us faded as we both laughed softly.

"Nope. It's called 'How Quietly Can You Come?'"

She made her lips into an *o* and her eyes went wide. "Sounds intriguing. How do we play?"

"Well," I said, my blood starting to heat as the game formulated in my mind. "You don't play. You lay back quietly while I do unspeakable things to your body to try to make you scream. The tricky part is if you wake up Dylan, the game is over."

Her eyes flashed and her nipples peaked beneath her thin T-shirt. "So how do I win?"

"You win by letting me make you come over and over again, and staying quiet enough that we can keep going." I yanked my shirt over my head and dropped it on the floor before reaching for my belt buckle. "What do you say, Addison? You want to play with me?"

Her gaze flicked below my waist, and I didn't need to look down to know that my cock was already as stiff as fuck and clearly outlined through the denim. This had seemed like a great idea when I'd first thought of it, but now I wondered how the hell I was going to keep quiet when I already wanted to howl like a fucking animal at the thought of being buried inside her again.

"Yeah," she whispered, reaching out a hand to trace

my shaft through my jeans. "Yeah, I wanna play."

I unbuckled my belt and unfastened my jeans, stripping them off in one motion. The boxers were next but I left them on, needing something between us, no matter how flimsy. As wild as I felt, I didn't trust myself not to abandon the game before it even got started.

"Your body is like a statue," she whispered, her gaze trailing over me, leaving a path of fire in its wake. "Hard and gorgeous."

Her hands drifted down her own body, her fingers busily working the leggings she was wearing down her thighs. When she was done, she was completely bare from the waist down, and I groaned as I caught sight of the thin swatch of hair that led to her pussy. Her long, toned legs still held on to a kiss of late-summer sun, and I imagined them wrapped around my neck.

"Fuck, you look so good, Addison."

She settled back against the pillow and gave me a shy smile. "What now?"

That was a great question. Especially when I wanted to do so many things.

"First things first. In order to keep things fair and to make sure you let me do my work undisturbed, I'm going to have to restrain your hands."

Her eyes went wide and her pupils dilated. "Restrain me? Are you sure that's necessary?"

"Nope," I said, shaking my head. "Not at all, but when you decide to create a game, you can make up the rules. I'm in charge this time."

I bent to slide my belt from its loops and then stood, gripping the leather in my hands. "Scoot down," I instructed, my voice already gritty at the thought of what was to come next.

For a second, I wondered if Addison was going to back out. The way that pulse in her neck was beating, there was no question she was interested, but being restrained required a level of trust I wasn't sure I'd earned yet. Especially after the way I'd treated her that afternoon.

My blood sang when she slowly scooted down and lifted her arms over her head without prompting. "Like this?"

The move hitched her little T-shirt high, baring her

flat stomach and just a glimpse of the underside of both breasts.

Nice.

"Yup," I said, setting one knee on the bed as I looped the brown leather around her wrists. It took almost a minute to get them bound tight and to fasten the belt to the slatted headboard.

I leaned back to admire my handiwork with a growl. "This is a fucking wet dream come true," I admitted, staring down at her, drinking in every inch of her with my gaze. I straightened and made my way to the foot of the bed, every nerve ending alive with anticipation.

Goose bumps rose on her legs as I gripped her ankles and slowly slid them apart. "Remember the rules, Addison. Quiet, or it's game over."

She nodded, her eyes hot with desire as I settled between her thighs. Her pussy was already slick for me, the pink flesh gleaming in the soft light, and I trailed a single finger over her in the lightest of touches. She stiffened and let out a tiny puff of air.

"That's good," I murmured, nodding. "So quiet,

love." I traced gentle circles against her heated flesh, barely grazing the skin but moving closer to her clit with each pass. Minutes passed as I blew against her gently, treating her skin like a watercolor canvas. When I finally passed over her clit with my thumb, she groaned and then bit her lip.

"Perfect," I muttered, wanting nothing more than to dive in and eat her alive, but knowing I had to resist. I repeated the touch over and over, barely grazing the bud of nerves, watching as her muscles tensed and trembled.

"Max," she whispered, arching closer. "Harder. Please touch me harder."

I wanted to. Lord, did I want to, but for the next hour, I managed to resist in an effort to wring every moan, every groan, every sigh from Addison's body.

By the time I finally slid my cock deep, she'd come four times and was primed for another orgasm. I was so far gone, it took no time at all for me to join her as she tightened around me. I exploded inside her, her name a hoarse groan ripped from my lips.

The sounds of our harsh breathing filled the room as the roaring in my ears finally quieted a few minutes later.

My bones were like liquid as I rose to my knees and gently unfastened the belt from Addison's wrists. Red marks blazed her golden skin, and I bent to kiss each one.

"Did I hurt you?" I asked, running my thumb over the offending marks.

"No," she said with a breathless snort. "I almost hurt me, though. I couldn't stay still at the end there, and think I nearly tore the headboard off." She brought her arms down and curled them around me, pulling me against her for a quick kiss. "The marks are nothing. They'll be faded by tomorrow and totally worth it."

"In that case, maybe we should plan a weekly game night." My blood was already heating up again at the thought, but her bright smile flickered for just an instant.

"Okay, but next time, I get to make up the rules."

As long as she was still here with me, I could live with that. I stretched onto my back and she curled against my side, fitting her body to mine like a puzzle piece. My whole life, I'd never known I could love another person this completely. Suddenly, in a matter of less than two months, I'd found two people who had become integral to my happiness . . . vital to making my world right.

Addison shifted closer, wrapping one leg around my hip as she drifted off to sleep. I made a mental vow to do everything in my power to erase the last of her doubts and make sure this was how I went to sleep every night. With her by my side.

Because anything less would be half of a life.

Chapter Twenty-four

Addison

Light streamed in, and I let my eyes flutter open with a sigh.

I'd been in the middle of the best dream. Max and Dylan and I were at the beach making a sand castle together. It was a beautiful breezy day, and I felt the most perfect sense of calm.

Now, in the harsh light of day, that sense of calm was fading fast. I peeked to my left to see the other side of the bed empty, save for a note on the pillow.

I rolled over and breathed in the scent of Max's pillow as I snagged the note and unfolded it. My lips split into a grin at the sloppy writing.

It's a beautiful morning and we were starving so we walked over to the bakery to get chocolate croissants. Daddy said you looked too pretty to wake up, but we're gonna bring you one back, so don't eat.

Love,

Dylan

A rush of emotion welled up and I slumped back against the mattress with a groan. Last night had been amazing. The thought of Max's magical hands all over me made my thighs quiver. But there was no denying that it had only made me even more afraid of what was to come. I knew I was going to have to respond to his proposal one way or another, and soon. I'd managed to avoid it last night, but I doubted we'd get through another day without it coming up. Especially after the intimacy of last night.

I glanced at the clock and a sudden wave of panic washed over me. Dylan and Max would probably be back any minute. So I did the only thing that made sense. I threw on a pair of flip-flops, brushed my teeth, and ran.

An hour later, I was sitting across from Lara in what used to be our favorite coffee shop as she stared at me from across the table, something akin to horror in her eyes.

"Did you at least text him and let him know you were leaving?"

I fidgeted, tracing shapes into the foam of my latte as I shook my head. "No, not yet."

"But you said the note he left said they'd be back shortly and were bringing you breakfast. Don't you think he might wonder where you went?"

She wasn't being mean, exactly, but I couldn't help getting defensive.

"I guess so, but I wasn't really thinking about that. I just knew I needed to get out of there, fast." I groaned and bent to bury my face in my hands. "Lara, I swear, it felt like the walls were closing in on me."

"Because of the proposal?" she asked, her tone gentling.

"No." *At least, not entirely.* "I know that I want to be with Max and Dylan. I've never wanted anything more. But when I think of Greg, I can't help but question my own judgment. What if I say yes, and this all turns out the same way?"

"By the same way, I'm guessing you don't mean by Max telling you he's gay, after all?" she probed, pausing to take a sip of her macchiato.

I almost laughed out loud at that, but the sheer vastness of my freak-out held me back. "No, Max is definitely straight. I mean, what if he decides I'm not what he wants, after all?"

Lara shook her head firmly. "You know, the other day when you told me that you weren't sure he wanted to be exclusive and all that, I was nervous for you. But now? Girl, I am all about it. You know why?"

I shook my head slowly.

"Because he asked you to marry him. He wants to commit to you. Surely he wouldn't do that if he wasn't sure what he wanted. Heck, from what you said, he didn't even ask the mother of his child to marry him. Seems like a pretty big step for a guy who hates the idea of commitment." She threw her hands up. "And as far as Greg comparisons, let me ask you this. Has Max asked you to give up your career dreams to support his?"

I tugged absently on my bottom lip and shook my head.

"Has he asked you to give up your time or your money to invest into his business? Or told you that spending time with your friends when you could be working on said business meant you didn't care about him?"

"No." In fact, Max encouraged me to take time off from caring for Dylan to get some "me" time and meet up with Lara at least once a week. And when we'd talked about the fact that I hadn't gotten my degree, he'd encouraged me to go back to school if I wanted.

"So, Greg asked for everything. What has Max asked for?"

When she said it like that, the comparison between the two seemed silly.

"Just my love," I admitted softly.

"As it should be," she said with a smug nod.

I drank down the rest of my latte, my heart pumping as hope began to spread through my chest.

"Well?" Lara demanded, glaring at me. "What the hell are you waiting for? Get your ass back there and get that big sexy man to put a ring on it before I try to steal him from you."

I stood and wrapped her in a weepy bear hug. "Thank you. You always manage to get me back on track when I'm spinning off the rails. Love you, Lara."

She pulled back and gave me a laughing shove. "Sushi's on you next week. Now, go! My break's over and I need to get back to work."

The trip back home was interminable, and I considered calling Max and telling him everything I was feeling over the phone. Instead, I stuffed it into the center console and recited the words in my head, determined not to screw it all up this time like I had when he'd first asked me and I went totally tongue-tied.

* * *

When I walked in the door an hour later, the sound of Max singing Dylan's favorite song in his rusty baritone rang in my ears, and a feeling of pure joy washed over me. If I could just do this the right way, this could be my life.

I stepped into the living room, and Max turned to face me from the spot where he and Dylan were sitting on the floor.

"Hey," he said, his tone guarded. "We were getting a little worried, but I didn't want to bug you if you just wanted to get a little space. Everything okay?"

Greg would never have cared or worried about bugging me or about me needing space. If he wanted something or needed me, that was all that had ever mattered. The fact that Max had clearly wondered where I'd gone but had considered my needs before his made me even more sure. I wanted so badly to rush over there and wipe away the worry lines bisecting his forehead, but I stopped a few feet away, blowing Dylan a kiss as she burst into giggles.

"Everything is perfect. Or it was, at least," I said, shrugging. "Until I nearly screwed it up by being a chicken. I love you. I love Dylan, and I don't know why I even hesitated. Ask me again, Max," I murmured, nerves bouncing around in my stomach like Pop Rocks. "Please."

My fears that he would hesitate or flat-out refuse disappeared as his jaw tensed with determination and his eyes blazed with passion. He rose onto one knee and slowly reached into his pants pocket.

"I'm sure glad you came back, because while Dylan and I were out getting croissants, we passed a jewelry store, and she wouldn't be deterred." He tugged a box free and opened it with a click. I stared down in awe at a stunning diamond solitaire winking up at me. It was simply perfect.

"Addison, since the day we met, you've blown me away. From your wit and humor, to the sweet way you interact with Dylan—" The baby cooed and looked up from the blocks she'd been playing with to give Addison a grin. "From the way you attack life and make me want to be a better man, to the way you've rocked my socks off in bed. I can't imagine anything that would make me happier than if you would agree to be my wife."

Sincerity shone from his face as he gazed up at me, and I didn't waste a second. I dropped to my knees beside him and shoved him back onto the rug, peppering his face with kisses.

"Yes! Yes, yes, yes!" Dylan squealed, scuttling over to join me, slobbering wet baby kisses all over Max's face.

"Assin!" she hollered, clapping her hands as we all laughed.

Max gripped the nape of my neck and dragged me close for a second, peering deep into my eyes. "I love you so much." He took my hand and slid the ring onto my finger with a satisfied nod. "And now you're mine, forever and ever."

I stared down at the ring, the sense of rightness settling over me almost overwhelming. "And you're mine."

"I wouldn't have it any other way," he murmured, trailing his hand over my cheek gently.

"Well, I mean, you are mine, but I meant it in a more immediate sense," I said, happiness bubbling over into a fit of giggles.

"What's that supposed to mean?" he asked, cocking his head suspiciously.

"It means it's game night, buddy. And I'm the master of ceremonies. Better make sure you drink a lot of water and maybe do some carb loading." I patted his cheek and then stood, lifting Dylan into my arms. "You're going to need your strength."

I sashayed away, adding a little swing to my hips as I went into the kitchen in search of chocolate croissants.

"Addison?" Max called, his voice laced with laughter. "Should I be afraid?"

"Oh yeaaaah."

Epilogue

Max

One year later . . .

"Please give it up for the bride and groom as they dance for the first time as husband and wife!"

I pulled Addison into my arms and held her close, pressing my face into her neck to breathe in her scent. All the fussy business was done now, and I got to spend the rest of my night with my best girls, surrounded by loved ones and friends.

For the life of me, I couldn't recall why I'd been so averse to the concept of marriage. The last year with Addison and the baby had been the best of my life, and I thanked the fates every day that we'd found each other.

Addison had decided she'd like to spend the first few years at home raising Dylan while I worked, and she'd picked up some classes at the local university so that when Dylan hit kindergarten age, she could teach at the local elementary school. We'd already both decided that we'd love to add more kids to the mix, especially now that Jenn had signed over her rights to Dylan, and Addison had officially adopted her. She'd been concerned about trying before the adoption was final because she never wanted Dylan to feel like she was less ours than any other kids we might be lucky enough to have.

For the past month since the papers had gone through, we'd been having the time of our lives "trying," and I couldn't wait to add another bundle of joy to our little family.

"Love you, Mrs. Alexander," I murmured into her sweet-smelling hair.

"Love you too, Mr. Alexander," Addison whispered back, her breath against my ear making my pulse jackhammer, just like she'd known it would. She flattened her breasts against me and tightened her hold around my neck.

"You're a very naughty wife," I muttered, clutching her hips with a chuckle.

Suddenly, there was a chorus of "awwww" followed by roaring laughter, and I straightened just in time to see Dylan sprinting toward us, her dimples flashing. She'd apparently had enough of her flower girl's dress and had managed to get it halfway off as my mother chased her, smiling ruefully.

"Sorry, she's a slippery one."

"It's okay, Mom, we've got her," Addison said with a beaming smile as she bent to scoop Dylan up into her arms. The baby wrapped one plump arm around each of us.

"Dylan dance too?"

"Of course, sweet pea," I said, swaying to the music.

"Thank you, Max." Addison's gaze tripped from me to Dylan and back again. "Thank you for inviting me in and for letting me become Dylan's mom. She's a gift to me, and so are you."

My throat went a little tight at the swell of love rising inside me. "I didn't even know how empty my life was until you both came into it."

"It's perfect, and so was today. Exactly what I wanted. Family, fun, and full of laughs and love," Addison said, her soft smile growing wider with excitement. "And tomorrow, Hawaii! We get to spend a week in paradise."

"I'm already there, baby," I murmured, crushing them both closer. "I'm already there."

Other Titles in the Roommates Series

Smith Hamilton has it all—he's smart, good-looking, and loaded. But he remembers a time when he had nothing and no one, so he's not about to mess up, especially with his best friend's little sister. That means keeping Evie at arm's length . . . even though the once pesky little girl is now a buxom bombshell. A sexy blonde who pushes his self-control to the limit the night she crawls into bed with him.

Evie Reed knows she's blessed. She has an exclusive education, a family who loves her, and a new job managing social media for her family's lingerie company. But she wants more, like a reason to wear the sexy lingerie herself, and she has just the man in mind to help her with that. She's crushed on Smith forever. Surely, tricking her way into his bed will force him to see her in a new, adult way.

Except that when Evie's plan leads to disaster, she and Smith must decide. Should they ignore the attraction sizzling between them, or become play mates and risk it all?

ROOM

The last time I saw my best friend's younger brother, he was a geek wearing braces. But when Cannon shows up to crash in my spare room, I get a swift reality check.

Now twenty-four, he's broad shouldered and masculine, and so sinfully sexy, I want to climb him like the jungle gyms we used to enjoy. At six-foot-something with lean muscles hiding under his T-shirt, a deep sexy voice, and full lips that pull into a smirk when he studies me, he's pure temptation.

Fresh out of a messy breakup, he doesn't want any entanglements. But I can resist, right?

I'm holding strong until the third night of our new arrangement when we get drunk and he confesses his biggest secret of all: he's cursed when it comes to sex. Apparently he's a god in bed, and women instantly fall in love with him.

I'm calling bullshit. In fact, I'm going to prove him

wrong, and if I rack up a few much-needed orgasms in the process, all the better.

There's no way I'm going to fall in love with Cannon. But once we start . . . I realize betting against him may have been the biggest mistake of my life.

SOUL Mate

From New York Times Bestseller, Kendall Ryan, comes a sexy new standalone novel in her Roommates series.

The smoking hot one-night-stand I was never supposed to see again? Yeah, well I might be pregnant, and he's my OBGYN.

Acknowledgments

There are so many wonderful people who support me in this writing journey. Most of all, I want to thank you, the reader. Thank you for picking up this book and giving it a chance. I love being an author, and I couldn't do it without wonderful readers like you.

My husband is a constant source of encouragement, and for his love and unwavering support, I am so grateful. Thank you for being my rock, babe.

I owe a tremendous amount of thanks to the following ladies—Danielle Sanchez, Pam Berehulke, Rachel Brookes, Natasha Madison, and Alyssa Garcia. A giant thank-you to each of you. I'm so blessed to have your support and encouragement.

About the Author

A New York Times, Wall Street Journal, and USA Today bestselling author of more than two dozen titles, Kendall Ryan has sold over 2 million books and her books have been translated into several languages in countries around the world. Her books have also appeared on the New York Times and USA Today bestseller lists more than three dozen times. Ryan has been featured in such publications as USA Today, Newsweek, and InTouch Magazine. She lives in Texas with her husband and two sons.

To be notified of new releases or sales, join Kendall's mailing list: **www.kendallryanbooks.com/newsletter.**

Or visit her online: **www.kendallryanbooks.com**

Other Books by Kendall Ryan

For a complete list of Kendall's books, visit:

http://www.kendallryanbooks.com/all-books/